# CHAOS DEMONS

THE SECRETS GODS KEEP: BOOK 2

TESSA COLE

CLARA WILS

Gryphon's Gate Publishing

Chaos Demons



This is a work of fiction. Names, places, characters, and events are entirely the product of the author's imagination or are used fictitiously, and any resemblance to persons, living or dead, actual locals, events, or organizations is coincidental.

Gryphon's Gate Publishing
550 King St. N.
PO Box 42088 Conestoga
Waterloo, ON
N2L 6K5

Print ISBN: 978-1-990587-31-3

# ANAIS

LIFE WAS PERFECT... ALMOST.

I mean things were certainly a lot better than any other time in my life. I had three amazing — and powerful — men who wanted nothing more than to please me and give me lots of orgasms.

And I loved that part, even if those three guys rarely got along.

They were all just a little too alpha male and there was a reason there was only one alpha in a pack.

My family life was also going well. My uncle Don had regained his memories and was once again a financial genius, day trading and investing and doing a lot of other things I didn't really understand. While Reia — my youngest daughter — and I were even getting along... most of the time.

She was teaching me to play chess, and I was

surprised to learn I liked it and wasn't half bad at it, even if I still couldn't beat her.

To top it off, my job at Elysium — a high-end club for daemons — was going well, and my manager, Harmonia, was becoming a great friend and sounding board as I tried to figure myself out, something I was still struggling to do.

Having accepted that I was indeed a daemon — a lesser celestial being that was one step down from a god — I wanted more than ever to know who my parents had been. I felt as if knowing that would tell me so much about who I was.

And I really needed to start figuring out who I was, because my guys were starting to not-so-subtly hint that they wanted more from our relationship.

Except how could I give more if I hadn't figured myself out yet? How could I love them if I didn't even love myself?

If I could just understand and love myself, then perhaps I could — terrifying as it was — love someone else and accept that they could love me. *Then* my life would be perfect.

But I wasn't there yet.

"Penny for your thoughts?" Grey asked, startling me from my reverie.

He set a large mug of steaming tea on the table beside my chair in my front room and straightened, rigid and refined. He'd taken to his role of butler in our household with vigor and had even bought an old-timey butler uniform: a black three-piece suit with a gray vest and a jacket with tails.

This man was a billionaire but he'd given up all of that to be my live-in man-servant. And his new uniform was of course perfectly tailored and did *everything* to set off his masculine beauty, accentuating his broad shoulders and narrow waist.

Except even though he was playing the role of servant, he couldn't hide his commanding nature. Authority just radiated off of him like a heady musk. The dark stubble of a trimmed beard framed his square jaw, and his well-tanned skin and thick, black hair added to his exotic look.

Then there were his eyes: so deep a girl could lose herself in them, falling for an eternity into those sable depths. Ever since he'd come to stay with me, the soul-sucking void which had resided in those eyes had vanished, but still, they were luscious pools of dark intensity, and I loved staring into them.

He'd asked me a question...

"Oh... ah... my thoughts?"

I blinked up at him. Currently, my thoughts were all about tearing that fancy suit off him like a lollipop wrapper and licking the sexy core beneath. "Ah... nothing really."

"Still wondering about who you are?" he asked, as perceptive as ever.

I sighed, squirming, unsettled despite the large and comfortable chair where I'd curled up. "Yeah."

He laid a reassuring hand on my shoulder. "You'll get there. You've got many years ahead of you to figure it out."

Right… I was immortal… Maybe?

I wasn't really sure at this point. I was a daemon now, technically a "daemon lady," since I had two aspects: sex and healing, and the guys — and Harmonia — had assured me that I was immortal… *now*. Although none of them could explain why I'd come into my powers so late in life.

I was nearly forty. For most daemons, their powers showed up in their teens. But I'd lived as a human for most of my life until just recently when I'd discovered I was a daemon and my life had been turned upside down. Still, I wouldn't really know if I'd stopped aging for a few more years.

"Yeah… right," I said, agreeing with him, although it was obvious I didn't sound certain about it.

Grey smiled. "Anything I can get you? Anything you need?"

*You, naked in my bed, giving me multiple screaming orgasms,* my horny self purred in my head.

*Down girl!* I chided myself.

Though… I did want that. But I didn't want to take advantage of Grey's role in my house. He had certain nights where he'd be with me as a lover, not a butler, but the rest of the time, he simply wanted to be near me. Apparently, I filled some void within him. And the nights I wasn't with him, I was busy with either work or one of my other guys.

“No… I’m good for now. Thank you, Grey.”

He bowed and left, smiling.

What a man.

The front door opened, and Reia came in, huffing and sweating from her after-school run with our new pet, Kerberos.

“Hey, Mom,” she called over to me. “I’m gonna jump in the shower then do my homework.”

She undid the leash and Kerberos sat, panting happily next to her. Luckily the horse-sized hellhound could alter its form to fit its environment, so now he just looked like a large dog, even if he still seemed huge next to Reia’s petite frame.

“You around tonight?” she asked. “Want to play chess?”

“I’ve got to work, but not until eight, so I’ll have a bit of time to play.”

Reia smiled and jogged up the stairs. Kerberos followed.

Grey had brought his “puppy” when he’d moved in, and the hellhound had taken to Reia almost instantly. I’d been surprised when Reia had, in turn, taken to the beast.

I hadn’t thought she’d be interested in a pet, especially a large, slavering, dangerous dog. But now they were inseparable, and thankfully Grey didn’t mind. He had other duties to attend to and was happy the pup was getting attention.

Reia, usually quiet and staid, had taken up jogging so

she could walk the hellhound. At least I didn't worry about her getting into any danger while running around the city. I was fairly certain having a hellhound as her companion was more than enough protection.

Life certainly had changed for me... in so many ways.

Donny, my uncle, ambled down the stairs a moment after Reia had gone up and asked, "Have you seen Grey?"

"In the kitchen making supper," I guessed based on the noises and wonderful smells wafting from the back of the brownstone.

Uncle Don whisked past me, but then returned, backing up slowly. "Ah... Anais... how would you feel if I was... out of the house more?" he asked, seeming a bit hesitant.

I shrugged. "This *is* your house, not mine. You can do what you like." I wasn't sure why he was asking my permission.

He sat in the large chair next to mine. "Ah... good, because I was thinking of taking Grey up on his offer."

"Offer?" This was news to me.

Donny nodded. "Ah, yes, I couldn't recall if I'd mentioned it to you or not. Apologies. Grey and I got to talking about his businesses and finances and such and... one thing led to another and... he offered me a consultancy position in his banking division. I said I'd think about it, and I have, but... I should talk to you about it, too."

"Oh? Why?" I shrugged again. "You can do what you like. You really don't need my permission to do anything,"

I said, reaching over to touch his arm and offer reassurance. "I'm happy for you."

Donny smiled. "Thanks, and I know I don't need your permission, but you're an adult now. Even if this is my house, we both live here together. I just wanted to make sure you'd be okay with this."

"I am." Though, since I was curious, I asked, "What would you be doing?"

I didn't think I'd understand much of it, but I knew how much Donny loved to go on about his work.

Donny grimaced, with a bit of an overwhelmed look in his eyes. I found that odd. Didn't he want to take this job?

"Well," he said with a heavy breath. "Grey wants me to work directly with the CFO — that's chief financial officer — of Zagreus Financial and completely reform their investment practices. It's... a big job. I'd essentially be telling a few hundred banks how to do their job."

Ah... I understood the look now. Donny was a numbers guy, not a people person. Such a responsibility would probably weigh on him.

"It sounds like a big job," I said, leaving it open for him to comment.

"Yeah, really big. A bit overwhelming actually..." He trailed off. Then he smiled and seemed to regain some of himself with a deep breath. "But I've always liked challenges, and this would definitely be a challenge."

"It would," I replied. "But don't worry about me and Reia. We'll be fine. Go do what makes you happy."

His smile grew into a brilliant grin. “Yeah, I will, thanks. It’s still slightly terrifying,” he said as he rose. “This will be the first job I’ve had outside the house in... almost thirty years.”

“You’ll do fine,” I encouraged him.

“Thanks, Anais. I’ll go tell Grey I’m in.”

I was about to go back to pondering who I was and my life’s purpose when I heard a knock on the front door.

With a sigh, I rose and went over to open it. I’d been about to say, “hello,” but all I managed to get out was, “Hell...”

There, on the landing, was Eva, my middle daughter with her arms crossed, clearly upset, and surrounded by boxes and suitcases.

“Oh gee, thanks, Mom. Quite the welcome,” she said, glaring at me with silver-blue eyes identical to mine, daring me to challenge her. “I’m moving back in, and no... I don’t want to talk about it!”

# ANAIS

"EVA?" I BLINKED. "YOU'RE—"

"Please, save me the lecture, Mom," she snarled, brushing a copper-red lock of hair out of her eyes. "I don't want to hear it. I know you didn't like Trent and it turns out you were right. Well, now I know he's a creep and it's over and that's all I'm going to say about it. Now, can I come inside? It's cold out here."

"Allow me to help you with those," Grey said, swooping in to pluck up several of the cases, easily carrying them inside. "Which room will the young lady be staying in?" he asked me.

"Top floor, front room," I said, then turned to Eva to confirm. "You want your old room?"

"Yeah, whatever." She began picking up other items and ferrying them into the front room. I stepped back to let her do her thing, uncertain if she wanted help. "Who's the guy in the fancy get-up?" she asked.

"That's Grey, my..." *boyfriend?* Gods, that sounded so odd to say. Lover would be more accurate, but I wasn't going to tell my daughter that.

*Fuck-buddy?* my horny self asserted. *Private Dick? One of my daemon tri-fuck-ta?*

"He's my new... our... butler." Well, that hadn't come out right at all.

"Butler? We have a butler now? Swanky." Eva brought in the last of her things and I closed the door behind her.

"Are you... okay?" I asked tentatively.

She turned to look at me with an incredulous look. "You suddenly care?"

I winced. That had pierced straight to my heart. "I've always cared, Eva. I love you and I've always tried—"

"Tried to control me and tell me what to do and who I could see. That's not love, Mom. If you loved me, you'd leave me alone and let me see whoever I wanted to see."

And... there it was. It was like I was looking at my younger self: same eyes, same face, and the same attitude I'd had when I was her age.

I was pretty sure I'd said something like that to my adoptive parents growing up, and I knew exactly what she was feeling... and yet, I still didn't know how to reach out to her. I just wanted to keep her from making the same mistakes I had. And I'd made so many mistakes with bad boys in the past.

This was the problem with Eva. She was too much like me. You'd think that would mean we got along, but it didn't. We always seemed to end up fighting.

"I do love you, and I have no right to complain about who you see." I tried to salvage something from this conversation. I really didn't have any right to tell her what to do. She was eighteen now and technically an adult. Also... I was seeing three men at the same time right now so... yeah.

Eva gave a cocky grin. "Sooooo, if I wanted to bring home some fifty-year-old sugar-daddy to fuck me in the ass and make me scream so loud you'd hear me two floors down, you'd be okay with that?"

She always had to keep pushing.

"Yes?" I said, trying to be kind, while also trying not to imagine some creepy old dude doing nasty things with my daughter. But that "yes" had been more of a question than a firm agreement, and Eva knew it.

"Yeah right, Mom." She shook her head. "Look, I'm just home for a while. I'm sure I'll find another guy soon, then I'll be out of your hair and you can go back to your butler and whatever else you're doing these days."

She spun away from me, picked up her two cat carriers, and hurried up to her room.

Crap. I'd forgotten she had the two cats. What were their names again...? She'd named them after Egyptian goddesses: Sekhmet and Bast.

I guess we'd see how well they got along with Kerberos.

God, I hoped they didn't cause too much trouble.

Eva stormed up the stairs past Grey who was on his way back down.

"Trouble?" he asked as he grabbed more of her things.

I sighed. "With her... always."

"I heard that!" Eva shouted from upstairs.

Fuck.

I needed to be... somewhere else for a moment.

I grabbed my tea and went through the kitchen and back room out onto the small terrace that overlooked our small garden plot. This late into October almost everything was dead, but the colorful leaves that had fallen from the neighbor's trees created a patchwork blanket of reds, yellows, and oranges on the ground.

"Oh... Eva." I sighed heavily.

I tried to recall this Trent guy she'd been seeing. I'd only met him once or twice, briefly. He was older than Eva. She'd only just turned seventeen when she'd left with him, and he'd been in his mid-twenties. He was a biker... or something. His loud motorcycle had roared up outside whenever he'd come to pick her up and he had bad boy written all over him. Their age difference alone had made me cringe. She hadn't even met the *half-your-age-plus-seven* criteria for him. Though... I couldn't really use that anymore since my guys were all thousands of years older than me.

I sighed. Had I been wrong about Trent?

Although, from what Eva said, it didn't sound like it, and I was curious about what he'd done to piss her off.

Eva had a hair-trigger temper and was easy to set off, but I got the impression that whatever had happened hadn't been her fault. There were any number of things a guy could do to piss off his girl. Most of them were things I didn't want to think about in relation to my daughter. Then, I panicked for just a moment, wondering if Eva was pregnant.

I'd had my first child at seventeen, and I recalled being particularly pissy to my one remaining adoptive parent around that time.

When I'd finally told my father I was pregnant... he'd had a heart attack and died.

My mom had passed a year earlier, and I still believed it had been my horrible behavior that had driven my adoptive parents into an early grave.

But I was fairly certain Eva was on the pill. That much at least I'd been able to instill in her before she'd left home. Though, if she was like me, the pill was *not* a guaranteed countermeasure. I'd had two kids while on the pill. Now I insisted on condoms. That was especially true of my daemon lovers. Daemon men, it seemed, were particularly potent. Though that had meant getting special-order condoms for Ramsey because his cock was particularly... extraordinary.

If Eva *was* pregnant...

I sighed. If she was, she wouldn't tell me. I wouldn't find out until she was showing, assuming she was even living here by then.

I might never know if she found some other guy and left before her baby bump showed up. And I couldn't ask her. That would only start another fight.

I just had to hope that wasn't the reason — or part of the reason — she was home now.

Maybe I'd see if Reia had any thoughts on how to talk to Eva. My youngest child had always been more of an adult than I'd been. Perhaps she knew how to reach her sister. Though... to be fair, Reia and Eva had never really hit it off as sisters, so Reia might be as in-the-dark as I was.

"Fuck me," I whispered, leaning on the railing of the small terrace.

Then I stood up suddenly and turned to go inside. Eva may not want to hear much from me, but there was one thing I *needed* to tell her: that I was a daemon now and that she may be one too.

I left my tea — mostly untouched — in the kitchen and raced upstairs to her room, barging in... which in hindsight was a big mistake.

Eva lay curled up on her bed, clutching a pillow and sobbing. I stopped dead. Whatever this Trent guy had done, it had really hurt her. My heart broke. My poor baby! I—

"Get out!" she screamed at me, flinging the pillow at my head. I was so stunned that it actually hit me, bouncing off harmlessly before falling to the floor.

"Eva, there's something I need to tell you." I pushed ahead, determined to say this now and get it over and done with since no time was going to be a good time to tell her. "I'm—"

"I don't care. Fuck you! Leave me alone! Get out!" She

looked around for something else to throw at me and found the wireless bedside alarm clock. I didn't think she'd actually throw it, but then it was in her hand, and she was rearing back—

I backed out and closed the door quickly as the clock crashed into the other side of it.

"That went well," I whispered, grimacing through my sarcasm. "Time to talk to Reia."

# GREY

It seemed young Miss Eva was... very spirited.

I sighed as I cleaned up the fragments of a porcelain figure which had once been a fairy of some sort. Half the pieces had ended up on the front room's blue and beige rug, while the others had scattered in every other direction. I swept them all into a dustpan, then rose and glanced at Ana.

I hadn't said it to her yet, I didn't think she was ready to hear it, but in my heart, I knew I loved her and it hurt me to see her so upset.

Of course, I'd never loved anyone before in my life and had no idea what it felt like and had had to check with Harmonia about these strange, new feelings. But the undeniable conclusion was that I loved her.

I'd admired and respected people. I'd lusted and desired others. I'd even felt hints of affection for people, but nothing... nothing like what I felt for Anais.

Probably because, for all my previous relationships, my void had been there, tearing at me, distracting me from whatever else I felt. But since Ana filled my void, I was able to finally *feel* things. I could really and truly experience a full range of emotions and it was... wonderful! I knew love, and I knew I loved her, and I'd tell her... eventually. But now wasn't the time.

"Fuck me, Grey." She sighed running a hand up over her face and into her shimmering silver hair. "I just... don't know what to *do* with her!"

Ana leaned against a wall nearby, head back against the painted plaster, looking up at the ceiling. She crossed her arms under her magnificent breasts, emphasizing her bust. But that wasn't what captivated me in that moment. It was the pain in her silver-blue eyes.

"I tried to have Reia tell her about being a daemon and... well, you saw what happened."

I had. Young Eva had stormed downstairs to yell at Ana. The gist of her anger seemed to be that her mother wasn't "man enough" to tell her about this herself. Also, there seemed to be a fair amount of confusion and consternation. She still didn't believe what she was being told and thought it a "sick joke." She seemed to think her mother was "punishing her" for the time she'd spent away, living with her boyfriend.

"I try telling her the truth, and she throws my favorite figurine at me. Except I'm sure when she learns the truth, she'll yell at me for not having told her everything. I can't win with her!"

"I know a daemon who can fix this," I said as I held up the dustpan with the remains of the shattered figurine. "I'll have it repaired in a day or two."

As for what was happening with her daughter... I wouldn't be much help. I'd never had a child. I knew nothing about parenting and the care and time that went into it. After meeting Ana, I thought it might be something I'd want. I got along well with Young Miss Reia, or so I thought. But with Eva... I wasn't so sure anymore.

There was also the added matter of a bubbling turmoil in Eva that I felt *very* keenly.

She had an aspect that was bursting to get out. Yet from what I'd felt, I doubted it was sex or healing. This was more a roiling tempest of rage, which made me wonder where she might have acquired this new aspect.

I didn't know who her father might have been, but from what Ana had said, she was fairly certain he'd been human. That meant any aspect Eva possessed would be from Ana, and if so... that meant Ana was far more than just a daemon or daemon lady.

She was a goddess.

Except I couldn't be sure, which was just another mystery surrounding Ana.

I'd suspected for some time that Ana might be more than just a daemon lady. I just didn't know how to tell her, because it didn't make any sense. Gods were primal forces. They didn't forget they were gods. And as far as I knew, no new gods had been born in the last few decades.

So if she were that powerful ... why hadn't she — or

anyone around her — known or sensed what she was before now?

I laid a reassuring hand on her shoulder but didn't know what more I could do at the moment.

Ana pulled her gaze down from the ceiling to look at me. My heart beat all the harder when those pristine silver-blue eyes locked onto mine and her silken silver hair shifted over one eye. Gods, she was the most beautiful being I'd ever met.

"I don't know what to say," I said honestly. Yet Ana should know... "I think part of Eva's anger is coming from a deeper place within her."

Ana quirked a brow at that.

"I think she has an aspect that is blossoming and it's filled with violence and distress. I don't know what it is, yet, but I feel like it's fueling her anger at the moment. There may be nothing you *can* do until she comes into her power and begins to control it. I'm sorry, Ana. I know that's not what you wanted to hear."

"You got that right." She sighed heavily and thumped her head back against the wall and returned her gaze to the ceiling. "Where would she get an aspect like that?"

*From you,* I didn't say. It was still a mystifying option that I didn't understand yet. I wouldn't say anything to Ana about it until I knew more.

"I... don't know," I lied. And on top of that, there was more bad news. "As Eva comes into this aspect, if she doesn't learn to control it, it'll spill over and affect those around her. We may all soon start feeling as angry as she is."

"Fuck me," Ana bit out. "This just keeps getting better and better."

I put the dustpan down and pulled Ana into my arms. Her body was so full and lush, soft and warm, I couldn't get enough of simply holding her.

She put her head on my shoulder and sighed, her arms circling me. Neither of us said anything since there wasn't anything to say. Our embrace said it all.

I kissed the top of her head, smelling her lavender and citrus shampoo, a scent that clung to her and defined her: soft yet bold and tangy.

*This* was where I needed to be: close to her, in her arms.

I'd happily give up all my billions to be with her... and I was starting that process already.

Some of my businesses I'd sell, others I'd hand off to those I'd hand-picked and trusted to run them. For a while now, I'd been hands-off with most of my businesses except for Elysium and my shelters. Those... I'd keep. The others I didn't want anymore. Depending on how good a job Ana's Uncle Don did with my banks, I might give them to him. We'd see. I didn't need any of that as long as I had this amazing woman in my arms.

"I'm here for you," I whispered. "I'll always be here for you, whatever you need."

"I know," she mumbled into my chest. "You're so wonderful, Grey, thank you."

Those words made everything in my life make sense, made everything... *right*.

The doorbell rang, but I held Ana a moment longer, not wanting to leave her warm embrace.

Except the doorbell rang again and again... and again.

"I... should get that," I whispered, slightly annoyed.

She released me slowly. "And I should see who it is."

We made our way over to the door together, but with every step, I felt a growing sense of dread. My daemon senses tingled and, as I opened the door, I knew who was on the other side.

I'd known her all my life, I knew her power, her *feel*. The door opened to a far-too-thin woman with jaundiced, sickly yellow skin, sharp features, hazy grey-green eyes, and hair that was half mat-black, half bone-white.

"Melinoe," I breathed, feeling the muscles of my jaw tighten. What in Hades was she doing here?

"Brother," she rasped.

"Brother?" Ana echoed. She looked from Melinoe to me. "You two don't look anything alike!"

"That often happens with daemons," I explained before turning back to my sister. "What are you doing here?" I hoped this wouldn't last long. The last thing this household needed was The Lady of Madness.

Oddly, Melinoe didn't answer me and instead looked at Ana with a sneer. "So... this is the slut that's tempted you away from your empire, your life. And she hasn't even dedicated herself to your greatness. She opens her filthy legs to two other daemon princes."

Fury burst to life in Ana's eyes and I felt a similar rage rise up within me. Except before I could rebuke my sister, she pushed on.

"I've come to take you home," she said. "I'm worried about you." There was an odd sincerity in those words that I'd never heard before.

"Piss off, you bitch!" Ana hissed and her control of her aspect started to slip, which meant that suddenly I was angry and aroused at the same time. "You have no right to come to my house and—"

"But this isn't your house, is it? It belongs to your uncle, who isn't even a daemon! What sort of worthless daemon whore can't even afford her own place?" Melinoe scoffed.

Her contempt reignited my rage, and I slapped her... hard, sending her reeling and forcing her to cling to the front stoop's railing to stop from falling down the stairs.

"You have no right to speak to Ana that way," I snarled. "Leave now or—"

"I'm not leaving without you, brother!" Melinoe roared in her rasping voice. "Either you come with me, or I'm staying here to keep an eye on you."

That wasn't going to happen. I stepped back, starting to close the door, but then Melinoe's aspect of madness fully unveiled and crashed over me.

It shouldn't have affected me. I was a stronger daemon than she was. But somehow her power hit me harder than my slap had hit her.

It only took me a heartbeat to figure out what had

changed, what was different. My void was gone, and it had probably countered and crushed Melinoe's power before now. Without it, I was vulnerable to the wild delirium she exuded.

Stunned and struggling to breathe, I staggered back, watching Ana reel back as well. My mind spun into delusions and mania, fears and foolishness.

Melinoe walked into the house, striding between us. "Yes, I think I'll stay for a while and make myself at home."

"Like hell!" Ana bit out, seemingly recovering from the madness far faster than I was... which was impressive. "Get out. Now!"

"Where's your hospitality? I'm your lover's sister. Shouldn't you invite me in?"

"Fuck off!" Ana hissed. I felt something spark to life inside her, a flicker of some new aspect which felt a lot like Eva's.

Well, that answered one question... but opened up so many more.

Yet, as much as Ana was able to speak — which was more than I could do — she was still reeling from Melinoe's powers and not able to do much else.

Melinoe stared Ana down. "You have two choices, *girl*."

The way she said the last word spoke volumes. She knew Ana was a new daemon — far younger — and probably no match for Melinoe's powers.

"Either you let me live here and keep an eye on my

brother, or..." Her voice got deathly low and vicious. "I send this entire household into madness." She glanced at me. "I don't know what you've done to my brother, but it's clear you've weakened him. He shouldn't be affected by my madness. So, I'm going to stick around for a while and find out what you've done to him. And as long as I'm here... I promise to keep my aspect to a dull roar. But if you defy me... I'll send you over the brink into a true madness from which you and your family will *never* recover. So... which will it be?"

I reached out to Ana, a hand on her arm, finally able to find some words through the chaos in my mind. "Let... me talk... to her," I stammered.

Ana glared daggers at Melinoe then nodded to me and backed off, turning and walking away.

Melinoe released her power, and I shuddered in a long breath.

"What's happened to you, brother?" she hissed at me. "Why are you so weak? What has that whore done to you?"

"I love her," I whispered, and pushed Melinoe back to the door. "And if you call her anything other than a respectable lady one more time, I'll unleash my void on you, sister." I honestly didn't know if I could anymore. Though... if I got far enough away from Ana, I was certain my void would return.

Melinoe backed down a little. "Fine, brother. She's a pretty little... daemon *princess*." The way she said it, with her lips twitching and puckered, suggested the word tasted foul to her. "But I'm still staying. My aspect shouldn't have affected you like that. You've grown weak and I'm worried about you. Father has many enemies and if they knew you were like this..."

She wasn't wrong about that. My father was the king of an underworld — and a general bastard — and that meant I'd made more enemies than friends as a young daemon. And — until Melinoe had affected me just now — I hadn't realized how weak I'd become.

Without my void, I'd lost my main weapon against any vicious daemons out there who might seek to challenge a daemon prince. Just living without my void wouldn't be enough. I'd need to learn to control it.

I'd always had a *tenuous* control over it. I could unleash it on others or keep it restrained when I wanted, but I'd never been able to control how it affected me.

I knew now I couldn't just banish it. I needed to use Ana's calming influence to learn to control my void once and for all... and oddly, having Melinoe here would help. She'd be able to test me as I hopefully built up my strength and control.

"Let me talk to Ana," I said, my voice low. "I'll agree to have you stay here, but *only* if you agree not to use your power on these people at all. Only me."

"You know my latent abilities will affect them." She shrugged. "I'm just that powerful."

And she was. Not only was she — nearly — a match for me, but she was also linked to restless spirits. That meant that this time of year, as Samhain neared, she would get even stronger.

"But I agree to do nothing more than that." She gave a wide and wicked grin. She knew even her latent abilities would eventually drive this household mad, and I could only pray I'd learn to control my powers before that happened.

"Agreed," I said. "But Ana has the final say. Let me talk to her."

Melinoe kept that savage grin and shrugged. She knew she'd won.

I went to Ana, finding her in the kitchen, glaring at the kettle, waiting for it to boil.

"Get her out of my house," Ana hissed at me before I could say anything.

"You don't know how much I'd like to do that," I replied.

She turned her glare at me, probably sensing my hesitation. "But...?"

"But as much as I hate to admit it, Melinoe is right. I'm weaker now. Being close to you is wonderful, I don't feel my void at all, I can finally be happy," I said, hoping she'd understand just how significant that was. "But without my void, I'm vulnerable. I believe I can learn to control my void with Melinoe's help. *If* she stays. But you have the final word on that."

"Good."

"If she stays," I continued, "she's agreed to keep to

herself and help me develop my power. She's also agreed to be... reasonable and genial with you."

Ana raised an eyebrow at me.

Yeah, I wasn't sure I believed that either, but I had to hope because I didn't want to have a fight with Melinoe right now. "If she isn't, then you can tell her to leave."

Ana gave a grim smile at that. "Fine. As long as she remains civil and helps you, she can stay. But anything beyond that and she's out. She can have the back room on the top floor and she's to remain in her room unless it's time for a meal. At meals, she's not to speak at all. You can do whatever work you need with her up in her room. Those are my rules."

I nodded. Seemed fair.

I went back to Melinoe and explained the terms.

She shrugged. "Agreed." Then she seemed to soften a little. "I *am* worried about you, brother, truly."

I didn't doubt that. Melinoe had always been just a bit *too* friendly with me and overly concerned for my well-being. It wasn't uncommon for Greek daemons to mate with their siblings. Horny uncle Zeus had tried to fuck pretty much everyone... and everything. But that was *never* going to happen between me and Melinoe. Still... the way she laid a hand on my chest and looked up at me, all demure and yielding, made me think she was still trying.

She could try all she wanted. It wouldn't change how I felt.

I sighed.

Things were about to get a lot more complicated around here.

My fears were confirmed that night. Melinoe's aspects were madness and nightmares, and despite that she was on the top floor and I was in the basement, she still somehow got into my dreams. I dreamt of Ana yelling at me, furious. She said she hated me, that I was nothing to her, beneath her, worthless and that she had tired of me. Every word was like an arrow to my heart. She told me to leave and never return, that she couldn't stand the sight of me. She slapped me and pushed me out the door and I crumpled into a heap as my void writhed to life within me.

I woke in a cold sweat.

I needed to get my void under control and get Melinoe out of here... now!

Rising, I made my way up the many flights of stairs. There was no time like the present to begin. I suspected I wouldn't be getting a lot of sleep in the days to come, and if I wasn't, then neither was my sister.

# FEN

"GODS, IT'S *SO* GOOD TO BE OUT OF THAT HOUSE!" ANA breathed as we walked through Central Park.

The air had just a hint of bite to it, but the sun was still warm on my skin, and with the leaves in their autumn glory, it was a perfect October day.

I couldn't have gotten luckier with the weather when I'd suggested I meet her at her house and we walk across town to my restaurant for lunch, which was good because she desperately needed the time away.

"Between Eva and Melinoe, that house is a warzone. Everyone's walking on eggshells, but even the sound of cracking shells seems to set people off." She sighed. "But... I'm going to forget about all of that and focus on you." She looped her arm around mine, leaning into me in a wonderful way that made my cock sit up and take notice and my heart thunder. "Now... tell me something, anything to get my mind off of all that."

Where to begin.

"You're stunningly beautiful today," I whispered.

She wore a long-sleeved, body-hugging black turtleneck above a flirty, flared, bright red mini-skirt, and black, soft-suede, knee-length boots. It was a casual but sexy outfit, exemplifying everything that was Ana.

"That's a good start," she said snuggling closer to my side, both of her arms wrapping around my arm. "Tell me more."

"You smell like lavender and lemon, and your skin is soft and smooth and perfect. Also... your feet, they're perfect," I added. "A lot of women have... ah... not-so-nice feet, but yours are delicate and perfectly formed."

"That's... interesting. Go on."

"Your lips are like delicate rose petals, soft and velvety, and kissing you is like diving into a world of soft warmth and delicate passion."

"Ooooh, wow, okay," she said, her voice breathy. "I'm guessing we're going to skip lunch and go straight to *dessert* yet again?"

I laughed. It had become a thing between us ever since our first outing. "Dessert" meant using our mouths to taste all the sweetness of each other, and so far, in the three weeks since I'd met Ana, we'd kept ourselves to oral sex and some manual stimulation. I'd wanted to take it slow with her, get to know her before we finally broke the seal on penetration.

And a big part of me did want to skip lunch and go straight to "dessert." My beast was roused by her aspect, becoming agitated and active, and it wanted to mate with her, consume her, dominate her.

The odd thing was Ana's voice also soothed my wolf in a way I'd never encountered before. Whenever she spoke, the beast became as mild as a puppy, content and quiet.

I hadn't understood it at first, but I was pretty sure I did now. My wolf *knew* Ana was its ideal mate, and her aspect of sex got it extremely wound up, needing to be with her. At the same time, my wolf also recognized her as a true companion, and her voice — the expression of her true self over and above any daemon aspects — calmed it. It was one of the reasons I also *knew* I had to be with her. No one affected me like she did.

And that meant that before *dessert*, I wanted an appetizer of a different sort.

"Ana... can we... talk?" I asked, a bit hesitant to bring it up, given how rough a time she'd been having at home.

"Aren't we talking?" she said with a bit of a giggle. That sound filled me with joy. She was feeling better, happier.

"I want to talk about... you... about... your quest to find out who you are."

"Oh?" She didn't entirely pull away from me, but she inched away a little to look up at me with her stunning silver-blue eyes. "You do?"

I smiled reassuringly. "I want to help you."

"You do?" she repeated with a surprised smile.

I laughed. "Yes."

I didn't explain why in that moment because my reason was selfish. Ana claimed she wasn't ready for love, for a deep relationship, because she didn't know who she was. Whereas I desperately wanted to have a much deeper relationship with her.

I loved her. I wanted her to be happy, and by helping her figure out who she was, I hoped I'd achieve her goal... and mine.

"I've had some thoughts," I said, "if you want to hear them?"

"You have? Oh... sure!" She leaned into me again, making my wolf sigh with contentment.

"I know you want to know who your birth parents were," I said. "But I think you can know who you are without that. If you know who they were, all that really tells you is who *they* were. You've spent your entire life without them. They didn't influence your upbringing in any way. They're just... genetics. And knowing your genetics doesn't really tell you who you are on the inside."

She sighed. "I'm listening," she said with a hint of coolness to her voice. She hadn't liked hearing that, as I'd suspected, but I pushed on.

"I think the best way to know who you are is to simply list things you know about yourself and see what that tells you," I continued.

"But I feel like I know so little," she replied, her voice suddenly small as her grip around my arm tightened.

"I think you know more than you think," I told her. "Give it a shot. What do you know about yourself?"

She sighed. "I know I'm sexy, but then again, I'm a sex daemon, so I don't know if that counts."

"Oh... it counts, trust me," I replied, waggling my eyebrows suggestively at her, making her giggle.

"Good to know." But her mirth slipped away and she blew out another breath. "I guess... along those lines, I blossomed early and I know I was drawn to bad boys and they were drawn to me. At least, that's how I used to be. I don't think you're a bad boy. You're one of the nicest guys I've ever known, even if you have a world-ending beast within you."

"Thanks," I whispered, touched that she saw me for *me* and not for the monster inside me.

"And I guess if we keep on with my aspects, well, I've never had a cold or a broken bone in my life and I've always healed quickly." She drew in several long, deep breaths. "But... that's all I can think of. Both of those seem so superficial. I'm looking for who I am at my core. All that inner-most, dark, and messy stuff."

"Want to hear what I know about you?" I asked.

"Ah... sure?"

"I know you're a mother." I paused after saying this, to see if she had a response.

"Well, yeah, of course," she said, her tone brushing off that fact.

"Don't you think that's an integral part of your life, of who you are?"

She was quiet as we walked, then replied, "Yeah. I guess it is. I'm a mother."

She still didn't sound convinced.

"You're also a lover. I don't just mean *my* lover. I'm thinking more in the terms of lover as opposed to fighter. You take care of people. You took care of your children, and your uncle when he had dementia. I'm sure part of the appeal for any guy you've been with was a sense that you'd take care of them too. You tend to people's needs," I said. "I think it's what makes you such a good bartender. Ah... that's another thing you are: a server. You are really good at helping others. It probably goes hand in hand with tending to their needs. Does any of that ring true for you?"

She was silent, staring at the ground, and I could only see her silvery hair as she leaned her whole body against me.

"How did you get so wise?" she asked softly.

I laughed. "I've been around for a while. You start to get a sense for people after your second or third century among humanity."

"Right. I... I think a lot of what you're saying is true." Oddly she sighed heavily, seeming defeated. "But if so, why couldn't I see any of that in myself?"

Ah. That's why she'd been so quiet.

"Introspection isn't easy for a lot of people. Sometimes it takes an outside perspective to see things. That's what therapists are for."

"You'd make an excellent therapist."

"I've already got two careers, I'm good."

She laughed, light and free, thankfully brightening the moment.

"I think if you use my list of *things you are* as a starting point, you can probably start to see others in your life," I suggested. "And once you've got a long list... well, then I think you'll have a pretty good picture of who you are and what you want. If not, then maybe try to order them. Which ones do you want to be more of in your life? Which ones are most important to you? Something like that."

"Yup, sexy and wise, I... you're amazing Fen, thanks for this. You've really helped."

She stopped suddenly and pulled me toward her. Her arm slipped up behind my neck as her head tilted up and she drew me down to her. Her lips parted almost as soon as we touched, instantly going deep and needful as she pressed her body to mine, letting me know we'd definitely be skipping lunch.

I wrapped my arms around her and pulled her closer, her glorious, soft curves pressed against me. Everything about her turned me on: her vivacious spirit and lush body, her soft lips and deep probing tongue, her unique silver hair and eyes, soft skin, and her warm heart.

We were both a little breathless when she drew back. Though she didn't go far. Her lips brushed mine as she whispered, "I think it's time you devoured me. Wolfy."

I couldn't agree more.

But we were still too far from my apartment in the Bloomberg Tower.

I almost threw caution to the wind and plucked Ana up, so I could leap over the rooftops to get there quicker... but didn't, and we settled for a cab.

Except our desire had built to such an unbearable degree that by the time I closed the door to my apartment, I couldn't control myself. With an inhuman grunt, I ripped off my shirt.

"Fuck, that's sexy," she breathed, her eyes going wide as she took me in.

She stepped in and slid her hands over my chest and shoulders as she pressed herself against me and rose on her toes to whisper in my ear, "I'm not wearing any panties."

Then she licked my ear and stepped back. For a moment, I lost control and my wolf surged forth with all its bestial desire. I quickly reined it in but not before my cock had torn through my pants, ripping the waistband and sending them to my ankles.

"Fuck!" Ana yelped.

"Don't mind if I do," I growled, stepping forward and out of my ruined pants.

Easily, I picked her up and she wrapped her legs around me. The motion lifted her skirt, and the wet warmth of her pussy slid over my length.

With a growl, I hurried to my bedroom, tossed her onto my bed, and pulled a condom out of my nightstand, rolling it on in a flash.

Her eyes lit up, her cheeks flushed with desire, and she released a strained mewl of need.

"Are you ready?" she asked, breathless. "I am!"

She squirmed her way out of her top, revealing a lacy bra that barely contained her full breasts. At the same time, she opened her legs, her skirt pushed up and away, but not quite revealing her pussy.

I allowed myself to get lost in the throes of my wolf's desire, needing her now now now, and grabbed her legs. With a jerk, I pulled her to the edge of the bed, sliding her skirt up more until I could see her glistening folds.

There was no petting, no foreplay, and no subtlety when my wolf was in charge. We'd spent the entire cab ride all over each other and we were both more than ready for this. So I bent over her, lifted her hips, and thrust my aching cock into that moist slit.

She gasped, then moaned as I lifted the rest of her off the bed, pressing her to me, feeling the weight of her driving my cock deep into her core. With a groan of pleasure, she wrapped her legs around me again, her arms behind my neck, licking my chest and then my lips, and I turned and pressed her back to the wall, locking her in place. I planted my arms to either side of her head as I rocked my hips, pounding my cock into her slick depths.

Growling, I captured her lips with mine, attempting to devour her in only the best way, and she matched me, just as voracious in her need, sucking and consuming me back.

Her moans grew louder, hitching around her ragged

breath, and her hips crashed into mine with the same raging need that boiled within me.

Then she let out a shuddering moan into my mouth. Her release rushed around my cock, her canal tightening around me, pressing and clutching, dragging me closer and closer to the edge.

But I clenched my teeth, fighting to hold it back. I wanted to be in control when I came, not caught up in my wolf's hunger.

I tore one of my hands off the wall and raked it down her body, ripping off her lacy bra and grabbing her soft breast, her achingly hard nipple digging into my palm. I kneaded hard, making her canal twitch with aftershocks and she shuddered and gasped into my mouth.

Fuck, I was close... so very close, and I was quickly losing control of my wolf.

I hauled my mouth off hers, met her heated gaze, and barked, "Talk!"

A shiver rushed from her pussy up her body, tipping her head and rolling her eyes back. Another orgasm rushed over her, squeezing me tight, and I sucked in deep breaths, desperate to hold on.

"I want you to come," she moaned, her voice raspy with need. "Oh, gods yes!"

The sound of her voice eased my voracious beast, if only a little.

She shuddered and gasped again, strong aftershocks crashing through her, threatening my control but also helping me to hold on.

I'd regained enough of myself to savor every inch of her, the press of her soft body and the milking pull of her pussy.

Hel, it felt so good and my wolf howled inside me, desperate to fully fuck her with all his passion and ferocity.

My cock swelled, painfully close to a release.

Not yet.

I couldn't finish yet.

Not while my hold on my beast was tenuous.

"I can't stop coming on your fucking amazing cock," she moaned. "Please come, my beautiful wolf. Fill me with your hot—"

Her words tamed my wolf, but were too much for me.

I came... hard, roaring as I unleashed my torrent within her and she trembled through another release.

"—Ohhhh yeeeeessssss!" she cried. "Fuck, yes. That was so worth waiting for!" She shivered again and gasped, biting her lip.

I still couldn't talk, but I nodded as I filled the condom and my release oozed out around my cock, leaking out to drip over my balls and run down my legs. I didn't care. Like she'd said, this was totally worth it.

"You can throw me up against a wall and take me like that any time you like," she breathed, her words helping to soothe my wolf, which was rumbling with contentment now.

"That... was just... the appetizer," I said, my voice gruff. "We haven't even gotten to the main course yet."

Her eyes lit with passion.

"I don't know, I'm pretty... *full* already," she said, her gaze sliding down my body to where we joined, my cock still rigid within her.

I chuckled and pulled out of her quickly. "How about now?"

I tossed her back onto the bed, making her whimper, her gaze still heated and needy.

"Yup," she said, her voice breathy as she slid her fingers down to her clit and stroked it. "I want more. What's the main course?"

"You," I growled, rushing in and pushing her hand out of the way to claim her sweet, soaked folds with my mouth.

# ANAIS

My body quivered with bliss from Fen's savage, dominating, against-the-wall fuck. His cock had felt perfect inside me, filling me with pounding heat and quickly spiking my pleasure to oh-my-gods overwhelming levels, and now I was buzzed, feeling satisfied and loose... and still achy with need.

Thankfully he hadn't been able to wait to have me again, and his rough tongue, lapping over my pussy, was quickly stoking my fire back to blast-furnace levels. This man knew how to tongue-fuck a woman!

I tangled my fingers in his thick blond hair and pressed him close, my legs on his shoulders and my hips tilted to give him the best angle. My clit was raging, pounding with every rapid beat of my heart as he swirled his tongue and flicked over it again and again and again.

Another release crashed through me, this one sudden and hot and leaving me more desperate than before.

He eagerly lapped at my molten heat as it poured out of me, drawing out my release until I was a quivering, twitching, moaning mess. I was barely able to breathe and every muscle in my body had gone limp.

Slowly he drew away, a self-satisfied gleam in his eyes.

*Wicked, wicked wolf,* my horny self thought with her own self-satisfaction. *What a big tongue you have.*

Big indeed.

Which made me think of his cock, so big and hard it had torn through his pants and boxers, shredding the fabric as it burst forth.

I'd never seen anything so miraculously sexy in my life!

I turned to Fen to admire his stunning body, giddy at what was next, when I realized I still wore my skirt and boots.

Those definitely had to go.

As if hearing my thoughts, he reached for my boots and slowly pulled them off. Then he undid the buttons on my skirt and slid it off as well.

My breath hitched with anticipation, then released on a stuttering laugh when he knelt on the floor at the edge of the bed and started massaging my feet — which were hella-sore from those boots.

I melted under his firm strokes as they reignited the heat within me. I wasn't sure if I could orgasm from a foot rub, but I was already so high, that it was a serious possibility.

"Are you sure you're not the daemon of sex and foot rubs?" I asked through my moans.

He chuckled. "No, this just comes from years of experience once again." He tilted his head to one side. "Actually, I think it was my father who said that the fastest way to anyone's heart is through their stomach... or the soles of their feet. Loki gives the best foot rubs. Though, if he offers, don't take him up on it. He only does it when he's trying to manipulate people."

That made me think back to our conversation in the park.

"What do you know about yourself and who you are?" I asked.

"Hmmm, going deep are we?" He drew in a long breath. "Well... I know I'm supposed to help end the world. There are a few world-ending daemons out there and supposedly at the right time, we'll all join together and tear this place apart. I don't think any one of us could do it on our own. My wolf would make a royal mess of things and destroy a lot, but a solid coalition of gods could probably stop me."

That was my man, casually talking about how it would take a *gang* of full-fledged *gods* to *maybe* stop him. Wow!

"I know I love to destroy things," he continued. "But I also know that at first, I hated that about myself. I didn't want to be a destroyer. I wanted to be a builder." He smiled softly. "Then, one day, when I was a boy, I saw how a forest, ravaged by fire, was growing again. Destruction makes way for new life. I realized that by destroying... in the right way, I'm actually helping to create new things. That helped me get a handle on my urges to destroy."

Funny how a new perspective could change so much. I wondered if that was all I needed. Of course, it wasn't so easy to try and see something in a different way, not when you're stuck in the middle of it.

"I also know that I love food and using my mouth. I love the sensations of eating and all the glorious flavors." His gaze caught mine and he gave a wolfish grin. "You taste like honey and lemon. I don't know how that's possible, perhaps it's a sex daemon thing, but you're fucking delicious. I can't get enough of you."

Oh... wow.

Though... oddly I recalled the taste of his come, like sweet and salty custard. That... wasn't normal either. Perhaps it *was* a sex daemon thing? Now, I was curious. I shifted over to the edge of the bed.

"I want to taste you again," I said, rising to a sitting position as I looked down at his cock and blinked. "Oh... wow..."

He looked down. "Yeah. I made a mess. I can't help it when I'm with you."

The condom still clung to his semi-aroused length, the tip was bloated and full and it looked like his cum had pushed out and dripped over his balls and legs and floor and... everywhere.

Something he'd just said caught in my mind. "Wait,

were you not this... ah... potent when you were with other women?"

He scoffed. "Ah... well, daemon males are pretty virile in general, but... yeah... nothing like this. Though..." He frowned and pursed his lips in thought. "Long ago, I had a fling with Kostroma, a Slavic daemon of fertility, and it was similar with her." He blinked at me. "Do you think it's possible you have an aspect of fertility?"

Another aspect? More than two? "Wouldn't that make me a goddess?" I asked a bit hesitantly.

Fen's eyes grew a little hooded and heated. "You're already a goddess in my eyes."

Desire roared through me. I'd gone from almost zero — Who was I kidding, I was probably still at fifty — to a hundred in a second. One heated look and a sexy sentence and I was aching with need again.

"Get up," I demanded, my voice husky.

He stood as I slid off the bed and onto my knees before him. I seized the condom and pulled it off, tossing it into a nearby waste bin, then I slid my tongue over his cum-soaked tip.

Yup, he tasted like custard, sweet and a little salty and just a little bit tangy.

I took him into my mouth, opening my throat to swallow him fully, my lips around his base.

He shuddered with pleasure, setting off an answering shudder within me, and I moaned around him. There was something amazing about having this powerful man's cock in my mouth and knowing I could bring him to his knees with pleasure.

I sucked hard, hollowing my cheeks as I pulled slowly back, cleaning off his length and swallowing his sweetness.

He moaned and watched me with hooded eyes as his breathing turned ragged, and his cock swelled and hardened, full and ready once again.

I smiled up at him, shivering with desire at the needful fire in those pale blue eyes. "Yeah, it must be a sex daemon thing," I addressed his comment from a moment before. "Because *you* taste like custard."

I slowly stroked his shaft, wanting to keep him at this state of arousal. He'd already given me multiple orgasms *and* a foot rub, the least I could do was return the favor.

"What do you want?" I purred, and he let out a low, throaty growl, sending chills rushing down my spine.

"I want to release inside you without being constrained. I want you to feel my hot cum pouring into you." And before I could say that wouldn't be possible it was condoms or nothing, he added, "I want your ass."

Oh...?

Oh!

*Hell, yes!*

More than a few of the bad boys I'd been with had wanted anal, and I'd learned it could be incredibly satisfying. Even just thinking about it, my ass opened a little, expectant, needy, and my breathing picked up.

"You're going to need a bit more lubrication," I purred.

"I have lube."

"I have saliva." I flashed him a wicked grin and slid his cock back into my mouth.

"Your idea is better," he grunted as one of his hands fisted my hair.

I slid over him, covering him with a slick layer of saliva while teasing him with my tongue. What I needed was a nice anal vibrator to get me loose for him, but again, just thinking about that seemed to open my rear entrance even more.

Because... right! I'm a sex daemon!

I focused a touch of my aspect around my ass — I was getting a lot better at controlling it these days — and it loosened with a surge of pleasure that left me breathless and trembling.

Oh, yeah, I was ready.

I was *more* than ready. I needed him. My whole body ached to be filled by him. I gave him one last wet thrust through my mouth, then pulled away and lurched around on unsteady legs. I bent over with my hands on the bed, and wiggled my butt at him,

He released a low guttural snarl and seized my hips.

Oh, yes.

One of his hands slid up my back to fist my hair, as he notched his cock at my rear entrance.

"Fuck, yeah," he groaned as he slowly pushed in.

Pressure and pleasure filled me, sending tingles

rolling up and down my body. He slid in, smooth and sensual, because of my saliva and my aspect.

This was going to be amazing.

When he bottomed out, his hips pressing against my butt, I surged more of my power, making myself tighten around him, drawing a low, throaty growl that only added to my heightening need.

"Gods, you're perfect," he groaned as he gave three hard, quick thrusts that stole my breath and made me moan like a porn star.

"Talk to me," he commanded, his voice low. "My wolf is about to take control."

His body shook as if he were trying to control himself, then he grunted, his wolf breaking through and he began to viciously thrust inside me, twisting my desire higher and higher.

I would have talked, but the words stuck in my throat from the intoxicating intensity of euphoria flooding me.

He felt amazingly huge in my ass, hot and firm and plunging so incredibly deep. Every impact jolted through me, rolling wave after wave of pleasure up my body to explode out my mouth with a breathy grunt.

*Yes. Oh yes!*

I moaned and pushed back against him, meeting him stroke for stroke. I drowned in sensations, spinning higher and higher, barely able to catch my breath let alone speak. But I wasn't scared of him losing control. I knew he wouldn't hurt me and I ached to feel all of his savage beast unleashed on me.

He let out an inhuman howl, his cock lengthening, growing even more rigid. His fingers on my hips became claws, digging into my flesh, and pain mingled with my pleasure as the true primal power of his beast claim me.

*Oh yes. Yes, please.*

I spun, my desire getting tighter and tighter, my body thrumming on the verge of breaking. It was too much. He was too deep, thrusting too hard. And it. Was. Glorious!

"Yes!" I cried out, as I came.

Stars exploded behind my lids spinning me around and around and around and for a moment I was floating in blissful darkness. I was light and pleasure, hypersensitive nerves all firing at once, stealing all breath and thought.

Then I became all too aware of his claws digging into my hips and his massive, steel-hard cock pounding into me. Pain cut into my desire and my pulse picked up with the fear that maybe he would hurt me.

"Please," I gasped. "I need you, Fen!"

And just like that his claws returned to normal human fingers and his cock shrank back to its normal, but still impressive, size.

He paused, still deep inside me, his breathing ragged. With a groan, he leaned over me, his hands sliding up my sides, drawing pleasurable shivers and wiping away the pain.

"Did I hurt you?" he gasped, his voice strained. "I... my wolf... I've never... felt..."

"I wanted to feel your wolf... just once," I moaned, my

body recovering quickly. "If pain was the price, then it was worth it."

At that thought, I sent a spark of my healing to my hips and cured where his claws had cut me.

"You're good?" he asked, his tone still wary.

"Very good," I purred and wiggled my ass, shifting him inside me. That spiked my residual bliss and sent an aftershock rolling through me.

"Your turn," I whispered. "I want to feel you lose control and claim me. *You*, not your wolf."

"As you wish." He chuckled, which turned into a growling moan. His hands slid under me, coming to clutch my heavy breasts, and he began to move again, slowly at first, but building quickly.

My breasts were already sensitive, my nipples ragingly hard and aching, and his hard-gripping fingers, squeezing my softness and pinching my nipples, added a touch of playful pain to my mounting pleasure.

This was exactly what I'd asked for, what I wanted.

"Yes," I breathed. I needed to keep talking to keep his wolf in check. "Squeeze my titties and hammer that amazing cock into my ass. I want to feel your hot cum filling me. Come in my ass, please!"

He drove his cock into me again and again grunting with each powerful stroke.

"Say… it… again," he snarled.

I didn't know exactly what he wanted me to say, but… I had a good guess.

"Gods, Fen," I moaned, my pleasure threatening to

take me over the edge again. "I need you to fill my ass with your hot, squirting cum!"

His hands quickly shifted back to my hips for more control as he ramped up his thrusting, letting out a long groan.

"Gods, yes!" he cried out before slamming into me one final time.

His cock pulsed over and over, pouring heat into me in waves, sending delicious, shuddering pleasure rolling through my body.

"Yes..." he hissed, even as his hands slid back up my sides, helping to lift me from my bent-over position until I was standing again.

I turned my head back, seeking his lips. His mouth slammed into mine, his kiss hungry and filled with need. His hands roamed my body, one sliding up to massage a breast, while the other slid down to my slippery clit, rubbing like he wanted to polish it to a gleaming shine. That, along with the throbbing cock in my ass, ramped up the rolling pleasure until I shattered again with a full-body orgasm.

I moaned and panted into his mouth, but he wouldn't let up. It seemed as long as he was coming, he wanted me to come too... and he came for a *while*.

He was making a mess again, his hot cum streaming down my legs, mixing with my own dripping juices, and his lips only released mine once he'd finally finished.

"Fuck that was... so hot," I whispered, my body trembling, my legs jelly.

"You're... so hot," he breathed. "I can't believe you let my wolf claim you. I can't believe I was completely out of control like that... then... I wasn't. Your voice... you are the most magnificent and mysterious celestial being I've ever known."

He had to pause, gasping as his cock gave a few final pulses, the death throes of our pleasure.

"Wow," I moaned, "such sweet words after a savage butt-fuck is a little confusing, but also... so very you, Fen."

I reached out with my tongue and traced his lips. His tongue lashed out at mine, and for a moment we played in the heated space between our lips.

Then my stomach rumbled... far too loudly, making me wince with embarrassment.

Fen only chuckled. "Why don't you have a shower and get cleaned up while I make us something to eat."

"Why don't you join me in the shower, and we'll eat after?"

He slowly pulled out of me, and I felt just a little hollow without him inside me.

"If I join you in the shower," he replied, "we'll never eat."

Yeah, I knew that.

I spun to face him once he'd pulled out and crashed my lips back to his. I slid my body against his, savoring the delicious feel of slick flesh against flesh, and his cock twitched. Even after all of that, he was still roused.

"I may be hungry," I purred, "but I don't want you to stop touching me and making me feel wonderful."

He gave a throaty chuckle. "Your call."

So, my grumbling stomach was forgotten as we slipped into a very steamy shower, where we got clean... then dirty, then clean again until the hot water ran out.

He gathered a few bits of food on a tray after the shower, and we lounged on his bed, naked and taking turns nibbling on each other and the food until it was time for me to go.

Except I didn't want to leave.

Fen was so caring and sweet and hot and sexy and... everything! And I knew home would be a mess. As much as Melinoe had been living within the terms we'd agreed on, her just being there was wearing on everyone. Her madness had subtly seeped into all of us. And with Eva's outbursts and violence, which also seemed to be affecting the whole household, it was pure chaos.

"I don't want to go," I whispered to Fen, feeding him a grape.

"I think Grey and Ramsey might complain if you stayed here forever." He fed me a small piece of strong cheese which melted in my mouth.

I sighed. Yeah, I had to consider those two as well. Grey was looking haggard, not sleeping well, if at all. Ramsey... I didn't want him anywhere near my house. His conflict aspect would only make things worse.

Still, I couldn't stay here forever.

We dressed and I mourned the loss of that lacy bra, even if I didn't regret how it had been destroyed. Then Fen drove me home in his sleek Porsche.

Even just sitting on the street, outside my place, I could feel the turmoil and animosity from within.

"Fuck," Fen whispered. "That's... intense. Sorry you have to go home to that."

So was I.

We kissed, lightly, gently, his lips speaking all of his feelings for me. I knew he loved me, even if he'd never said it. I hoped — given the start he'd given me on figuring out who I was — that I might soon be able to reciprocate those feelings.

Then I got out and trudged back into the warzone.

# RAMSEY

I WAS IN A FOUL MOOD AS I WALKED INTO MY UNCLE'S office. Ana had just called and delayed our night together... *again*. She claimed things at home were rough and she was exhausted. Yeah... exhausted by Grey most likely. I hated that he lived with her now. Sure, his room was in the basement, but still, if a few flights of stairs were all that separated me from Ana, I'd be in her room every night!

"Ramses. Sit." My uncle's deep, dominant voice tore me from my thoughts, and I closed the door to his office behind me and found a chair.

"Why did you call me here, Osiris?" I asked, watching the large form of the man opposite me.

A large frame, with wide, heavy shoulders was a hallmark of our family, and Osiris was the personification of the perfect, dominating man. He was a god in truth, no mere daemon, with aspects of rulership, death, rebirth, fertility, and agriculture. He was the king of the Egyptian pantheon and when he called, you came... which is why I was here. Though, I didn't really know why I was here other than that.

"I've felt a disturbance among the dead," Osiris rumbled in a heady bass voice. "Those already within the confines of the underworld are well, but those who linger... are restless."

I shrugged. None of my aspects had anything to do with the dead. "And?"

Osiris's dark eyes bored into me, his face a scowl of scorn at my indifference.

"And," he growled, "a restless *Lord of Strife*, isn't helping matters in the least!"

Oh.

"You're losing control of your aspect, Ramsey. I felt it long before you entered my office. I can't have The Lord of Strife stirring up trouble with the dead. I don't know what's going on with you, but you need to get your shit together. Calm the fuck down. Now!"

Because a god shouting at you to calm down was *such a great* way to calm down.

I ground my teeth, jaw twitching. My chaos bunched and tumbled, pounding within me and echoing out into the world.

"If you can't get your strife under control, I will," Osiris threatened. "I'll stash you in some forgotten corner of the underworld and keep you there. That's your other option. What will it be... nephew?"

The thought of being taken so far from Ana nearly broke my mind, I couldn't allow that. I needed her with every fiber of my soul. *She* was what calmed my chaos, but I hadn't been able to see her.

I rose. "I'll take care of it, Uncle. I promise."

"You'd better."

I turned to leave, but he spoke again. "I've got Anubis looking into what's riling up the dead, other than you, that is. Once you've gotten yourself under control, help him."

Gods, I hated when Osiris ordered me around.

"What's Horus doing?" I spat back, just a little too vehemently. I turned back in time to catch Osiris' heavy sigh.

"He's being a royal prick, as usual. Even if he *is* my son, you know I can't command another who possesses the aspect of rulership. The day he does anything for himself — or to help any of us — is the day the world ends."

Good to know Cousin Horus was still a do-nothing, entitled ass. It was a not-so-well-kept, shameful, family secret that Horus had insisted on being breastfed by Isis until well after he was a thousand years old. That poor woman loved and hated her son. The rest of us just hated the stuck-up daemon prince.

"Fine," I muttered.

"Good."

And that was that. I left and stalked down through the office complex to the parking garage and burned off far too much rubber from my Lamborghini's tires as I sped out of there. I had to see Ana... now... no excuses.

I made it to her place in record time, parking in the middle of the street because I couldn't find any spots at the side and I couldn't wait.

I flew up her stoop and pounded on her door until someone answered. My chaos was throbbing within me, nearly out of control.

"Ramsey," Grey said — even before he'd seen me — as he opened the door. "Now *really* isn't a good time, especially with your conflict raging like that."

"Ana cools my chaos," I bit out, barely able to speak. "I need to see her... now!"

I pushed past him. Grey was strong, but not as strong as I was, and I barreled through him... far too easily. The Lord of Conquest fell with a very un-daemon-like "ooof," making me pause and turn back.

I hadn't really looked at Grey until that moment and was surprised at what I saw. He seemed... weak. His skin was far too pale, and there were huge bags under his eyes. It looked like he hadn't been sleeping much... but then, I'd never sleep if I was in Ana's bed.

My rage exploded and I nearly ripped the daemon lord limb from limb in that moment. The only thing that stopped me was the thought of Ana. Not only would she kill me if I hurt Grey, but... I needed her, now!

Charging upstairs I kicked down the door to her room and barged in. It was late morning and it looked like she was just getting up. Sitting on the side of her bed, slightly bedraggled — but still gorgeous — massaging her temples. She wore a pair of silken shorts and a robust cotton sports bra. It was far from lacy lingerie, but it was still so very hot on her.

She looked up, shocked, as I arrived. She also looked like she hadn't slept much. If I hadn't been certain before that Grey was occupying all her nights — a breach of our agreement — I was now.

"Ramsey?" Ana groaned. "What...?" She seemed to slowly catch up with what had just happened. "My door!"

"It's what you get for denying me while fucking Grey every night!" I roared, my rage suddenly blossoming into a living thing around me. "I need you, Ana. Now!" I began undoing my pants.

"What? Fuck, no! Ramsey, it's too early for this. I'm not tired because I've been with Grey." She rose, but seemed a bit unsteady on her feet, still holding her head with one hand. "I'm tired because I work late, and I can't sleep with Eva and Melin—"

"It doesn't matter. I need you, Ana." I had my cock out and was stepping out of my pants.

But at the same time, my mind was growing... fuzzy.

Why was I here?

My thoughts grew hazy and confused, words shifting in my mind. I needed two ducks and a cow.

What... no. Ducks?

That wasn't it. Not duck... but... fuck.

Yes... I needed to fuck Ana now! But my lust seemed to be taking a back seat to a confused anger. My thoughts were skewed, but I stayed my course. I went to Ana and mashed my lips to hers.

Even if she was tired, her body still instantly responded to mine, pressing into me as her mouth opened, our tongues dueling.

I slid my hand down into her silk shorts and between her legs, stroking her clit until she'd grown wet. She moaned into my mouth, the sexiest sound I knew. I pulled back from our kiss, my cock so very ready. "I'm going to truck your grain south."

"Whhhhaaaat?" She blinked.

"No... I meant... fuck your brains out!"

Why was it so hard to think straight?

I knew Ana affected me, but she'd never addled my mind like this before. It didn't matter. Even just being close to her, made my chaos start to subside... though I was still furious for some reason.

I threw Ana onto her bed and was there an instant later, pulling off her sleep shorts.

"Condom!" she cried out. "If we're doing this, then rubber-up, big boy."

I paused. I hadn't brought one with me.

Fuck!

But... I think she kept some of mine in her nightstand and I quickly checked, relieved to find my specially-made, uber-XXXL inside. I tore into it and began to roll it on. My need was maxed out, I was so ragingly hard for her. My cock was so stiff it was painful. Yet, looking back at Ana, her pussy was only slightly moist. I'd need to get her a lot more aroused before I'd be able to get into her.

Fuck.

I knelt and mashed my mouth to her folds, sucking and licking her clit, driving a finger inside her wet warmth.

"I don't know where this is coming from, but it's certainly not the worst way to wake up," Ana purred, her hands stroking the back of my head.

I inserted a second finger, stroking her g-spot. She was so receptive, and it wasn't long until she shuddered through her first orgasm, her pussy flooding around my hand. *Now* she was ready.

I rose and pulled her toward me, lifting her hips to my cock, my tip slipping into her folds. Yes! Finally! I needed this. My chaos was simmering, and I knew if I could just come with her, I'd finally settle.

"What the fuck, Mom! Gross! Close your fucking door!" The voice behind me startled me... and surged my anger. Whoever this was, they were stopping me from getting what I needed. I pulled out of Ana and spun as rage consumed me. Yet my fury seemed to spike my passion as well, and a curiously powerful rage-orgasm blasted through me.

"Fuck!" I cried out in both dismay and bliss as I began to fill my condom. What was happening to me?

I didn't recognize the young woman in the doorway... although she had some of Ana's features, the same silver eyes and face shape, but her hair was copper-red. Her face contorted in horror.

"Ew! Gross!" she cried out. "Holy fuck, Mom, this is the third guy this week! You've got no right to dictate who I fuck while you're whoring it up with everyone on the block. And this one couldn't even wait before he blew his load. What sort of sick fuck factory are you running here?" The young woman stalked away.

I was stuck between arousal, rage, confusion, indignation, and shame.

I staggered back, falling against a wall, hitting so hard I dented the drywall. Despite everything that had happened, I couldn't stop coming, pumping that condom full.

Ana was up, finding her shorts and slipping them on. When she looked at me, her face was beet-red with shame.

"I… I…" She shook her head, raising a hand to her temple again as if she had a headache. "I don't know what's going on."

She grabbed a housecoat and threw it around herself before running out of the room. That left me half dressed, half-aroused, but fully disappointed and furious. My chaos roared to life within me, and I fell to my knees, then all fours as it overwhelmed me. I did the first thing that came to mind, grabbing my cock and squeezing. The pain cleared my head for a second, enough for me to stop my chaos from fully exploding into the world around me. I'd probably bruised my dick, but I hadn't started world-war-three so... that was a win.

I could barely do anything, chaos, rage, and confusion tore at me. I managed to stand and stagger into Ana's bathroom, finding a garbage can to dispose of my condom. Then I stumbled back into her room and found my pants. My head was pounding so hard, it was difficult to think straight.

Slowly, I lurched down the stairs and heard the shouting match before I saw it. Descending to the main floor was like walking into a warzone.

Ana was shouting at the young woman, who was throwing anything in sight and shouting back. My head swarmed with pain and discordant thoughts. I could barely understand what they were saying, only that they were furious with each other. Somewhere above me a dog barked incessantly, and cats yowled. This was a madhouse!

Then Ana turned to me. "You!" she spat. "Your chaos isn't helping any of this! *This* is why I told you not to come, you're only making things worse. Come back when you're able to drain away some of our chaos, not add to it." She pushed me toward the door. "I just... can't... right now. I'll talk to you later. I'm sorry, but you have to go!" She opened the door and pushed me out. It was a testament to how disoriented I was that she was able to manhandle me so easily.

I stood on her front stoop for a long moment, dazed and confused and still so very angry.

"Fuck!" I bellowed at the sky.

Then I stumbled to my car, only realizing once I got in, that my pants were on backwards and I'd left my boxers inside.

I had no clue what had just happened, but I knew one thing for sure: if my chaos had been stormy before... it was a class-five hurricane now. And without Ana... I couldn't think of any way to calm it.

# ANAIS

My head hadn't stopped pounding for days and I'd barely slept. Every time I closed my eyes, I had nightmares of creepy crawlies and inescapable violence. I felt — and looked — like a royal mess.

"You have to help me," I begged Harmonia.

I'd gone to see my gracious and helpful manager at Elysium even though I didn't have a shift tonight. I'd told her about everything that had happened over the last however-many days — I'd lost track — since my daughter and Melinoe had arrived. We were all run ragged, barely sleeping and constantly arguing. Even quiet and stoic Reia was at her wit's end. I'd left after I'd yelled at Grey for my tea being too hot.

I couldn't believe I'd done that.

"It's completely unbearable." I slumped in my chair. "And I'm utterly exhausted."

Harmonia blew out a long breath. "Melinoe is... not

an easy daemon to live with. Even if she is controlling her powers, anyone near her will still probably have nightmares and slowly go mad. I'm not sure what Grey was thinking letting her in." She shook her head.

"He said something about his void and being powerless around me and learning to control it." I shrugged. I couldn't quite remember now, muddled as my mind was.

Harmonia nodded. "Well, let me do this much for you." She rose and came around her desk to stand behind me. She put her hands on either side of my head and her soothing power flowed into me. My muscles unbunched, shoulders slumping, jaw and neck untensed and—

Wow, I really had been uptight.

"Gods, you're amazing, thank you!" I said with a heavy sigh. "At least I can think now. Although I don't know what to do about any of this. If I tell Melinoe to leave, I think she'll throw a fit and literally drive us all mad. And the way Grey looked when he asked for her to stay... I think he was truly worried about his powers. And I have no clue what to do about Eva. I haven't even managed to tell her she's a daemon yet, and according to Grey, she needs to know soon, because she has some blossoming aspect of violence or anger or something and it's spilling out of her like mine used to."

"Do you want me to come over and try to calm things?"

Yes. Yes, I did, very much.

"I can't ask that of you." I grimaced. "I don't even

know if it's within your power to get this particular household under control."

"Why don't I stop by tomorrow and see if there's anything I can do?" Harmonia offered.

Oh, thank the gods!

"You're a saint, thank you," I said, exuding gratitude.

My mind latched on to a part of what she'd said. Tomorrow... was a significant day... for some reason? A holiday? Even with a clear head, I was still a little confused as to what exact day it was. Then it hit me.

"Oh! Tomorrow's Halloween."

"Most daemons call it Samhain."

"Sa-win?" I repeated. I'd heard that somewhere before.

"It's a Gaelic harvest festival, a time when the barrier between worlds is thin and spirits sometimes return."

"That... actually happens? Spirits can return?" Would I be able to see my adoptive parents and apologize for how horrid I'd been as a teen?

"Yes, though humans can't see them most of the time."

"Oh." But... I wasn't human anymore. "Oh!"

"And yes, I don't mind dropping by. The festival doesn't mean much to me personally. We Greek daemons have a different celebration of the dead in mid-to-late winter. It involves a lot of wine and is a lot... rowdier."

"Oh." Still. "I really appreciate you doing this. You don't know how much it means to me."

"Well, I'm doing it for you *and* Grey. He's still technically my boss, and I wouldn't want him going mad."

"Oh, yeah, right." I drew in a long, deep breath. God, I could finally breathe. "Thanks again, for everything, I should probably go."

Now that I could think, I wanted to spend some time pondering what Fen had asked me, about that list of things I knew about myself.

I got up and made to leave, but asked, "Do you mind if I stay in the lounge for a bit?"

Harmonia laughed. "Need a break before returning home? Yeah, go ahead."

It was only early afternoon, and the bar wasn't busy, the lounge was mostly empty. I sat and took a small notebook out of my purse, finding the page where I'd jotted down what I recalled from my conversation with Fen and where I'd added a few of my own musings to the list as well.

At the top of the page, I'd written: "I AM" in big bold letters. Below that, so far, I'd listed:

- a mother
- a lover / sex daemon
- "beautiful" / sexy / "vixen" / "hot-as-hell"
- a caregiver / servant / server (bartender?) / helper
- healthy / a healer

That was all I had so far. Most of these I'd thought of because someone had called me something like that before in my life. So, I tried to think of other things I'd been called: ones that were generally positive.

I tapped my pen against my lips. Even with a clear mind... this was really hard.

I tried to think back to my school days. I hadn't been good at much, but had there been anything I'd done well?

Oh... right! I'd been invited to do some plays, not because I was a good actor — I wasn't — but because someone had said I was charismatic.

I jotted down "charismatic" next to "hot-as-hell."

What else?

I was certainly doing a lot of arguing at home these days... which reminded me of times when my girls had been younger and been teased or bullied. I'd felt a righteous rage and fought for them, seeking justice and equality from her teachers and other parents. The girls had hated when I'd done that, but...

On a new line, I added: a fighter for justice and peacemaker.

Something about that felt... right. I smiled.

Still, after another hour of pondering, I hadn't come up with anything else.

I put my notebook away and left. I had a few other errands I needed to run. The first... was to apologize to Ramsey for kicking him out yesterday. As much as his chaos had not helped the household in the least... he'd been right about one thing. I'd been avoiding him.

Things had been turbulent at home, and rough sex with him just didn't have any appeal at the moment. But... I could at least talk to him now and try to explain things. And if there was some less-rough sex thrown in... well I *was* a lover after all, so why not.

Yet, when I stopped by his place... he wasn't there. The doorman knew me and let me up, but after knocking on his door for ten minutes, I figured I'd missed him. It was the middle of the day. He was probably at work.

I was turning to leave when another man approached. He was tall, with dark skin and a wide smile. There was a certain overly-happy-to-see-me sparkle in his dark eyes.

"Hello!" he called to me. "Are you here to see Ramses as well?"

I got a strange feeling from him. I hadn't made the connection until now, but I felt this whenever I was near my guys or Harmonia.

"Are you a daemon?" I blurted out before it occurred to me that that was probably really uncouth and rude.

The tall, lanky man continued to smile. "Yup! I'm Anubis. Who are you?" He was just a bit too happy and reminded me of an excited puppy.

"Ana," I said. "Anais. I'm a... friend of Ramsey's."

"I'm his sort-of cousin. Well, I *am* his cousin, but I wasn't always. I was adopted, sort of. It's complicated." He'd reached me by then and looked at Ramsey's door. "Not home?"

"Nope."

Anubis nodded. "I'll wait." Then he looked at me and that wide smile spread wider still. "Has anyone told you you're stunningly beautiful? You must be a daemon of beauty, right? Am I right?"

"Sex actually, but that's close enough." I didn't know why, but I felt perfectly comfortable talking with this guy and telling him I was a sex daemon.

He grinned. "Nice! What pantheon are you from?"

"I… don't know? I was adopted and—"

"Oh… sorry, my bad, don't worry." He quickly changed the topic. "Since I'm going to stick around here, is there a message you want to leave for Ramses?"

"Ah… yeah, thanks. Just tell him Ana stopped by and wanted to apologize."

Anubis raised a brow. "*You* need to apologize to *him*?" He laughed. "Usually, it's Ramses pissing people off and needing to apologize. Yeah, sure, I can let him know."

"Thanks," I said, finding a grin on my face. Talking to this guy just seemed really easy. I was about to leave when I thought to ask, "What are you a daemon of?"

"The dead," he said with a nod.

I blinked. "Really? But… you seem so happy?"

His constant smile widened again. "Well… yeah. I help the dead cross over into the underworld. I get to meet all sorts of interesting people! If they're good, then I get to see them into the underworld, and if they're evil… I get to feed their heart to a ravenous beast. Isn't that cool? Also, if it wasn't for me, then this world would be filled with restless dead, which would be bad. So yeah, I like what I do."

Huh. All I could think to say was, "You do you."

"You too!" he said, and I left.

Well... that was... odd, but not in a bad way.

# ANAIS

My next stop was a bit of a strange one. I wanted to track down Trent, Eva's ex. I'd only had his first name to go by, but Grey was an excellent hunter and had ways of tracking down people, so he'd found me the man's work address; a motorcycle garage on West 47$^{th}$.

It was fair to say I stood out, walking into the small shop in my cream-colored blouse and black pencil skirt, and all the guys stared at me.

"Which of you is Trent?"

Several of them pointed to a back room, their eyes never leaving me as I made my way around parts and grease puddles. I didn't bother knocking on the door to the back room, since it was slightly open. I just pushed on through.

"Trent?" I asked even as I took in the room.

A startled man spun around to face me. He was in grease-stained coveralls, his face smeared with oil as well.

He was actually fairly handsome with a strong jaw, thick black hair, and bright blue eyes. And... the girl with him was attractive as well with a similar tanned complexion, wavy brown locks, large brown eyes, and a lush figure like mine, but probably a decade and a half younger. Then... there was the baby in her arms.

Suddenly I had a good idea why Eva had left.

I'd come here hoping to find out what had happened between him and Eva and perhaps convince him to apologize and see if she'd return to him. At this point, I just couldn't live with her constant arguing over everything! There was just no way to talk to her sensibly and I was at my wits' end.

But with the tableau before me, I got a pretty good picture of why she'd left: he'd knocked up some other girl and Eva had found out.

I turned to leave, without saying a word, when Trent sputtered, "Mrs. Baker?"

I paused in the doorway.

"Yes," I said, the word clipped.

"Ah... this isn't what it looks like," he stammered.

Yeah... right. How many times had I heard *that* line?

"She's my sister," he said earnestly.

I spun back to him, confused and horrified for a moment. "You knocked up your own sister?" Though even as I said it, I realized there were other options.

"What? No! That's not my kid!" He sighed, running a hand over his face, smearing more grease over his features. "Please... just let me explain. Eva never gave me a chance to tell her what happened."

Curious, I nodded. "Talk."

"Close the door?" he asked quietly.

I did, leaning against it with my arms folded under my bust.

He rambled off his story, keeping his voice hushed. "My sister, Lisa, was married to a douche-bag. He wasn't good to her and when it seemed like he might hurt their child, she took the kid and left. But her husband is also a powerful guy with friends in high places. She didn't know where to go, so she came to me. I've been keeping her here, in the back room to keep her safe. But... I couldn't tell anyone she was here. I told my guys her name was Lina, some girl I'd knocked up, and I couldn't say anything to Eva... but she must have suspected something and came to work and found us. I know how it looks, but I'm just trying to be a good brother!"

I sighed. That, unfortunately, made sense.

This guy actually seemed like a decent fellow. He had a business and took care of his family. Perhaps he wasn't such a bad guy after all. But I could see how always-angry-Eva might not see that.

"Do you love her?" I asked, then clarified, "Eva, my daughter?"

"I do!" he insisted.

"He really does. He can't stop talking about her and how he's so sad he lost her," Lisa piped up. "Other than motorcycles, that's all he talks about."

I sighed. There was no way Eva would listen to anything I said so...

"You need to tell her that. You know where we live, stop by and I'll let you in. Eva is a little... upset right now." Boy was that an understatement. "But I hope to any god that might listen, that she'll talk to you."

Trent beamed. "Really? You think she'd have me back?"

I certainly hoped so.

"Yes," I lied. I really had no clue at all whether she'd even listen to him, but I had to try.

He rose and came to me, making to shake my hand then thinking better of it, seeing how filthy he was. "Ah... thank you so much, Mrs. Baker."

"Ms. Baker. I'm not married."

"Ms. Baker, I really appreciate this!" He nodded like a fool — a love-sick fool, I realized — and couldn't stop smiling.

Gods, I hoped this worked.

I left his shop and did a few other bits of running around town, before finally, reluctantly, returning home.

I could feel the animosity and turmoil even just standing on the street outside. I went in through the downstairs entrance and slipped into the basement, hoping Grey might be there. Luckily, he was.

I caught him half-dressed, topless, washing his shirt, vest, and jacket, all of which had red stains on them.

"Is that blood?" I asked, worried.

"No, tomato soup. There was a bit of a row over

lunch." He sighed heavily. I could see how tired he was, and I knew he hadn't been sleeping, working with Melinoe all night long. Any normal man would have passed out from exhaustion long ago, but we daemons could keep going for a while it seemed.

"She needs to go," I said softly as I drew close to Grey.

With his shirt off and all his gorgeous, tanned, rigid muscles exposed, I couldn't help myself, I had to touch him.

I ran my hands over his torso, kissing his shoulder. "Melinoe is driving us all mad, and you know it. I know you said you need her to get your void under control. But... is she really helping? Because if she stays another week, I think we'll all go mad."

"I'd make better progress if I were rested." He sighed, shaking his head. "I'm still struggling."

He turned to me and caught me up in a sudden, heated kiss, his arms tight around me. I responded instantly, my hands continuing to roam his amazing torso as I opened my mouth to his and we lost ourselves in each other for a moment.

He pulled back and whispered, "When you're with me, near me, everything seems right. I... I don't want my void. I hate how it feels. But... if I can't learn to summon it at will, then I wouldn't be able to protect you or myself if anything were to happen."

"Do you... need some time... away from me?" I didn't want that, and I hoped that was clear from how I'd said it.

He shook his head. "No... maybe... I don't know. I

can't imagine not being close to you anymore. I just need to learn to summon my void when I need it."

"But… you also don't want to, because you hate how it feels, and that's making it hard," I finished for him, guessing how he felt.

He nodded.

I kissed the rock-hard muscles of his chest. "Well, you need to figure this out, Grey. Because I need you, but I can't live with Melinoe for much longer."

"I need you too," he whispered, lips brushing mine. They continued to brush mine as one of his hands began expertly undoing the buttons of my blouse. The other hand curved over my butt then began bunching up my skirt.

Heat blossomed in my chest, seeping into my limbs and sinking heavily into my core. From my aspect, I could feel Grey's passion pounding against me, into me, and it sent a shivering rush tingling through me. I'd given up on wearing panties since all it took was the slightest stimulation to get my pussy wet and ready.

I undid Grey's pants and slid a hand down to grasp his throbbing cock, stroking him gently as he removed my shirt and expertly unhooked my bra. He lifted me effortlessly and I wrapped my legs around him, shifting my hips so his twitching tip brushed my slick folds.

He brought his lips down to a breast, sucking hard on an already rouse nipple, teasing it with his tongue until it was achingly stiff.

I moaned, using my legs to lever myself up then down, dipping his cock into my raging heat.

With a groan, he grabbed my hips and slammed me down on him, driving himself deep inside me, his pent-up passion finally bursting from his control.

His lips found mine in a hungry, devouring kiss as if the damn on all his desire had shattered and he couldn't get enough of me.

Fuck! We'd forgotten a condom!

But I didn't want him to stop, not now. So... screw it... literally.

I ground myself against him as he drove into me with hard, short thrusts, seeking to sate our mutual, throbbing lust.

"Get off my brother, you filthy slut!" Melinoe's voice — and her power — slammed over both of us.

Impossible visions swarmed in my mind: Grey clutching his chest, having a heart attack, screaming as spiders swarmed out of his mouth.

I didn't know what Grey saw, but we both cried out and threw ourselves off each other. I stumbled and fell on my ass. Grey staggered back and swiped at something that wasn't there before crashing into a wall. He sank to his knees.

Melinoe ran to him and waved a hand before his face, whispering, "See me as her." She grabbed his cock, stroking it hard as she pulled Grey's face to hers for a hard kiss.

*Oh-hell-no!* That was not going to happen for... so very many reasons.

I rose, my vision still swimming with illusions. But it seemed her focus was on him now and I was mostly able to see the reality around me. I stalked to them, tore her away from Grey, and slapped her as hard as I could.

Melinoe crumpled to the floor.

"Take that, bitch!" I spat the words at her. "He's mine! And he's also your brother so... just... ewww!"

Melinoe didn't move, limp, but breathing.

I didn't think I'd hit her *that* hard. Kneeling, I checked her pulse, which was still strong. Apparently, I'd hit her hard enough to knock her out. I hadn't known I had it in me.

The visions were fading around me. Grey groaned as he seemed to come out of his madness. He looked at me and his sister. His gaze kept shifting between the two of us as he sighed heavily.

"You're right, she can't stay," he said, though he sounded a bit defeated.

"We'll find some other way to help you get your void back... when you want it." I smiled at him, hoping that would help cheer him up, but he just nodded slowly.

We dressed quickly, and Grey carried Melinoe up to her room. We packed the few things she'd brought so she'd be ready to leave when she woke. I didn't know how willing she'd be, but we'd find some way to make her get out.

Grey returned with me to my room. My door was still

broken, but we propped it in place and hoped that would keep everyone out. I tried to tease him into continuing what we'd started earlier, but we were both exhausted. In the end, we just held each other as we succumbed to sleep.

# IN CALVARY CEMETERY

*Nari draws deep breaths, filled with power. This is it. His time has finally come! The corpses around him are rousing, rising, and their strength lends him power. He hasn't felt this strong in several generations of those pitiful humans. Finally, the other daemons and gods will listen to him, will see and heed his power and grant him the place he deserves among them, no longer shunned, but respected.*

*"Rise, my minions," he hisses, raising his arms out to the sides, feeling their power combine with his, reaching a crescendo as some distant clock finishes the chime for midnight. It's now All Hallows Eve, and his power is paramount.*

*There's no sign at first, the graves are still. Yet Nari can feel the corpses moving, breaking free of their coffins and beginning their desperate dig to join him.*

*"Rise!" he calls out, as the earth over several plots begins to churn and sink, displaced by the emptiness below. From the*

*distance comes the sound of crashing stone as mausoleum doors and covers are broken.*

*The first few sets of hands break the surface, soon followed by the remainder of their bodies. Nari has tended them well. Some have been here for more than a hundred and fifty years, but they are intact and strong, a gruesome facsimile of life. No souls linger in these bodies. They're driven by the mystical energies of this day and the connection to the realm beyond seeping through the veil between worlds.*

*The first few bodies climb clear of the soil, as others, farther out, begin to break free.*

*"Rise!" Nari shouts, exultant, his rasping voice echoing into the night.*

*These millions of minions feed his aspect and he, in turn, bolsters them, a reciprocal relationship, feeding off each other and building a cycle of power that spirals to ascendant heights.*

*The dead rise, breaking free of their confines be that earth or stone, and walk once again. They swarm into the city, seeking the warmth of the living, driven to consume their blood. They have no minds of their own but are controlled by Nari, who is lost to his own power.*

*Some of the dead spread out into Queens, but many... most... head for Manhattan. There, Nari sends them. There... his brethren will witness his power. There, millions of humans will die only to strengthen his army. For every body that falls will rise again under his power. There will be no stopping the dead. For on this day, augmented by his minions... Nari has exceeded his strength as a daemon.*

*Today... Nari is a god!*

# RAMSEY

I COULD FEEL CHAOS MOUNTING. THINGS WERE ESCALATING quickly.

Anubis and I had been out seeking the source of the restless dead since I'd found him waiting outside my apartment that evening.

Anubis had given me the message that Ana had stopped by and said she was sorry. I had been happy to hear it and had wanted to go see her that instant... but Anubis had convinced me this mission was far more urgent and important than my love life.

Love...

After our first time together, I'd told Ana I loved her. The words had spilled from my lips before my mind had reeled them in. My heart had opened and gushed out through my mouth and stunned us both. Luckily, she'd played off my admission as: *I loved fucking her*, and I'd run with that because I couldn't believe I was truly in love.

I was the Lord of Strife.

I didn't love.

I fought.

Never before in my entire, very long life had I loved anyone. My family was distant, pursuing their own aspects. I respected them, but I didn't love them. And the women I'd taken to my bed had been a pleasant distraction, a release.

But I'd never before felt anything like what I felt for Ana.

My heart constricted just thinking of her. It was almost physically painful to be away from her. I couldn't think straight, constantly distracted by thoughts of this amazing woman. And... it was throwing my life into chaos.

I'd spent thousands of years getting my chaos under control. I'd worked hard to become a good man, someone who punished those who caused undue strife. Quelling the chaos in the world helped me control my own.

Between that and the release of my conflict through the underground fights, I'd been in control of myself for centuries.

But now it felt like everything I'd worked so hard to build was crumbling.

My chaos was reeling around me and I needed Ana. I felt at peace when I was with her. She had this strange dual effect on me, rousing my chaos with her intense aspect of sexuality, while at the same time, calming me.

That first time we'd been together, I'd lost control but

she'd brought me back. No one, other than her, had ever been able to bring me back from my chaos. And the times we'd been together since, I'd found I didn't need to hold back. I could let go of my control and ravish her, and my chaos wouldn't emerge because *she* was keeping it in check.

But I hadn't been with her in so long that I was beginning to feel lost and wild, senseless and berserk.

So... when Anubis and I got stuck in traffic trying to cross the Queensboro Bridge, I couldn't take it anymore. I got out of the car and just began stalking toward Queens with Anubis at my heels.

We didn't even reach the end of the bridge when screams tore at the night somewhere ahead of us. People ran toward us, panicked and I could feel raw chaos, like a wave, heading our way. I looked at Anubis, and he nodded. He felt something too.

"There are dead up ahead," he said over the uproar around us. "But I don't sense any souls."

We hurried against the flow of charging people until we saw them.

"Fuck me," I hissed.

They swarmed over cars and people in a wave of bodies. Any person they captured was bitten and drained, their blood flowing out of them.

"Vampires?" I hissed.

"No, they're mindless, not in control, seeking only to feed, more like zombies."

"Great, zompires, that sounds like fun," I said with a

huff as my chaos rolled off the undead and strengthened me like nothing I'd felt since the Mongols had swarmed over the world. At least I'd be at the peak of my strife when I fought these nasty things.

"I don't know how much help I'll be," Anubis said, concerned. "My sway is over souls. I have strength as a protector of tombs, to put right the desecrated dead, but... I've never faced *this* many undead before."

"Do what you can, I'll do the rest," I hissed, finally feeling like I had an outlet for my raging chaos.

My strength was enhanced to the point that I was able to pick up a car — holding it like a giant club — as the zompires drew near. I swatted a dozen of them off the bridge, then crushed another half-dozen with the make-shift weapon. Then I picked up another car and continued the fight.

But things got out of hand far too quickly. More and more zompires swarmed me. The first few were easy to keep away, one super-powered punch destroyed them, but as more came, it became increasingly difficult to even move as they pressed in around me.

I waved my arm killing five of them but even more took their place. They sunk their teeth into me, clawing and drinking. I hardly felt the pain, I was too amped up to notice, but the flowing blood did start to weaken me.

I destroyed dozens — perhaps hundreds — but it wasn't enough. More came and the next wave seemed even more powerful than the last, nearly as powerful as I was!

Anubis broke through to me, looking pretty rough himself.

"We can't stop them. We must flee!" he shouted, even as he tackled me, pushing me to the edge of the bridge. From there, the press of the horde pushed us over the side, and we fell into the East River.

As we swam to Roosevelt Island and I thought of my failure, my chaos rose even more. Crawling onto the shore, I couldn't stop shaking my head.

"What the fuck?" I hissed, furious with myself. "What was that? I couldn't stop them!" My chaos was near-to-overflowing and I could barely keep it in check.

Anubis sighed heavily. "Those things... they surged your chaos, made you stronger... but your chaos echoed back to them... made them stronger too. I could feel it. The stronger *you* got, the stronger *they* got, and there were far more of them than you. You'd never have won." He shook his head slowly. "You can't fight them, Ramsey, not until you get your chaos under control. You need to be able to use it without radiating it around you. As long as you stay as you are, you'll only make those abominations stronger."

"Fuck," I hissed. He was right. "Fuck!" I slammed my fist down into the rocks, shattering them with my newfound strength. "I need Ana!" I said, feeling desperate.

"Can she help you get yourself under control?"

"I... yes. Yes, she can."

"Then seek her out and do what you must. But return

as soon as you can. That wave of undead will be in Manhattan shortly. I'll do what I can to slow them, but I fear it won't be enough."

"Can't Osiris get off his ass and help? What's a god of the Dead good for if he can't control the fucking dead!"

Anubis nodded. "I'll contact him."

I rose and turned to him. "I'll be back as soon as I can." Then I dove into the East River.

*I'm coming, Ana, and I hope you're ready for me, because this time if we don't connect, the entire city might be destroyed!*

# ANAIS

I WOKE WITH A SCREAM.

That dream had felt... different. It hadn't been distorted and maddening. There hadn't been any creepy crawlies or delirium. No, this one had been clear... if horrifying.

It hadn't been spiders and bugs, but people... dead people. They'd been swarming over others, biting and drinking their blood, and seemingly getting more powerful as they went. Then, as the swarm passed, those they'd killed rose to follow them. It had scared the life out of me, and I woke in a cold sweat.

Grey jerked awake next to me, eyes going wide.

"A hunt is coming," he whispered before blinking and seemingly coming fully awake. "What did I just say?"

"A hunt is coming," I repeated.

"Fuck," he whispered. Then his brows furrowed. I could only just see him with the hint of light leaking in through my window from the street outside. "You couldn't sleep?"

"I had a bad dream, just woke up."

Grey nodded slowly. "I... did your dream involve a strange wave of the dead devouring others?"

I blinked. "Yes. How did you know?"

"I had the same dream." He began to rise, quickly. "Something is happening. I can feel it. I think you're feeling it too."

I turned on the bedside lamp and took just a moment to admire Grey's extremely-hot naked body. He slept naked because... of course he did.

Olive-tanned skin covered his tall frame. His muscles bunched and stretched as he moved, shoulders rolling, thighs shifting. Thick dark hair and that ever-present dark scruff of a beard framed his hard-edged face, which was a mask of concern. His sable eyes seemed lost in thought. Then... of course, there was the swinging length of man-meat slapping his thighs before he found his boxers and pulled them on.

I'd slept naked this time as well, we'd stripped each other — trying to rekindle our passion — but had just ended up asleep.

I rose, but something stopped me from putting on the blouse and skirt I'd been wearing, and instead, I went to my dresser and pulled out a pair of comfortable jeans and a black T-shirt. Then I went to my closet and pulled out a badass leather jacket, slipping that on over everything else.

Grey only had the pants of his butler uniform up here. He'd been washing the top pieces earlier. He had duplicates in his room, of course, but for now, he was topless and gorgeous.

Then his eyes caught me in my get-up and his breath hitched before he gave a soft laugh. "Is there anything you don't look good in?"

"I don't tend to look as good in brown or any shade of green. I stay away from earth tones, but other than that... nope."

He laughed outright. "Of course."

Then he came to me, three long strides across the room, and pulled me close in a ravenous kiss. I opened my lips as his tongue slashed across them, then met his driving need with my own.

He was so impassioned and — with my aspect — I could feel every ounce of it. He hadn't done anything more than crush me close to him and devour my mouth, but my aspect made sure I was ready for anything.

The shifting of our bodies against each other sent sparks showering through me, lighting an inner flame that quickly blazed over my skin and superheated my core. I was certain he felt my ragingly taut nipples even through my shirt and jacket, and he was definitely feeling my hips rocking against his lengthening erection.

But then he pulled away suddenly. "We... should... I... need to dress," he said, then quickly left, heading downstairs.

"What...?" I gasped after him, having not fully recovered my breath yet. "But...?"

I sighed. This was the downside to being a sex daemon. Men captured you and kissed you and got you raring to go because they couldn't help themselves, even if they'd been on their way to do something else... like get dressed and face some mysterious, unknown, spooky dream situation.

"Fuck me..."

*If only,* my horny self huffed, disappointed.

I made my way out after Grey.

Reia was peeking out from her room at the back of the house, Kerberos at her side. "Mom?" Her voice was hushed and I barely heard it from the other end of the long hall. She was fully dressed in sweatpants and a baggy sweater. "I... had a bad dream."

"People eating other people?" I guessed.

She shuddered and nodded. Then she ran to me, and I pulled her close. I guessed all of us daemons had sensed it.

Daemons...

Including Eva...

And Melinoe...

Even as I thought that, I heard footsteps above us, then coming down the stairs. Eva was still in her pajamas: a white, two-piece set with shorts and a supportive empire cami, fringed with lace under the bust. Whoever had bought that for her had put some thought into it, as it seemed to bridge that impossible gap between comfortable *and* sexy. Gods, she was far too much like me: an early bloomer who broke hearts left and right.

"Mom? Reia?" For the first time since she'd arrived, Eva's voice was soft, measured, non-hostile. "I... I heard you talking about... that dream...? What's happening?"

She seemed afraid, and fearing to break this fragile moment, I didn't say anything, just beckoned her down and she joined my embrace with Reia.

I held my girls close, wanting to keep them safe. But some part of me knew that if they were like me, their lives were going to be very interesting and potentially... very dangerous at times.

That made me hold them all the tighter.

"I love you both, so much," I whispered.

"We love you too," Reia said.

"What's happening," Eva repeated her question. "Why do I feel like I need to fight... everyone... all the time!"

I had an idea. "Come with me and I'll try to explain."

For whatever reason, Eva seemed to have lost her hostility and I needed to make the most of it while it lasted.

I brought them down to the main floor, into the kitchen, and found a nice sharp knife. Without any explanation, I sliced the blade across my palm.

For all the times I'd seen it done in movies, I'd assumed it wouldn't hurt *that* much. I was wrong.

"Holy fucking shit! Fuck, that hurts!" I hissed through clenched teeth.

"What are you doing, Mom?" Eva asked.

Reia, of course, was already several steps ahead. "Just watch."

I didn't need much impetus to heal myself, making the wound close quickly. That left my palm bloody, but I quickly washed that off and showed Eva the unblemished hand.

Eva blinked. "What the fuck?"

"Remember what Reia told you about me being a daemon and you and she probably being daemons as well?" Eva blinked at me, not getting it yet. "Well, one of my powers is healing. I can heal myself or others. It's messed up, I know, but it's true. I also have power over sex, but I didn't want to make my daughters feel horny to prove that one."

"You mean... that wasn't a joke?" Eva whispered.

"Nope." I met her gaze. "And I think you're developing some power around violence or fighting or something. As my daughter, you're also part daemon. I don't know where your aspect — that's what these powers are called — is coming from, but that seems the most logical explanation for what you're feeling. Also... we can feel it too. It's leaking out of you. You're making the rest of us restless and agitated as well. You're going to need to learn to control your powers... soon."

"So..." I could feel the moment slipping away as Eva's animosity bubbled up within her. "I'm feeling this way because of you? This is your fault?" Accusation flashed in her eyes.

I couldn't deny it. "Probably, yes, somehow. I'm sorry, Eva."

"Fuck sorry. Can't you... heal me of this shit or something?" she yelled.

"I heal physical wounds. I can't heal your aspect. You need to learn to control it."

Her face was slowly flushing with anger.

Reia sighed. "Since we're up, I'm going to take Kerberos for a walk. I think he's restless too."

"Don't go too far from home this time, okay?" I urged her.

"I'll stay close, just run up and down the street," she said with a nod, then left.

Eva was fuming. "Control...? How can I... I just want to... argh!"

"Ah... hey Mom?" Reia's voice carried back from the front room. "There's some guy outside."

Some guy? Reia knew Ramsey, Grey, and Fen. So... who would she call "some guy"?

I hurried to the door.

"Trent?" I asked surprised to see the man I'd spoken to that afternoon, Eva's ex.

"I... I've been thinking about what you said, Ms. Baker, and I couldn't sleep so I drove over here and was sitting outside, but then I saw lights coming on and... Oh... Eva!" He peered behind me.

I felt it before I heard it, the wave of fury which hit me from behind so hard, it nearly bowled me over.

"You!" Eva roared. "What are you doing here? What

do you mean *you've been thinking about what my mother said*... Mom... did you see this creep! I can't believe this!"

Well, if our neighbors hadn't been awake... they were now.

I pulled Trent inside, but even as I did, a beast leap down from the roof of the house across the street. It was half-man, half-wolf, and shimmering with power, radiating a need to consume and destroy.

"Fuck! Fen?"

# FEN

A HORRID HOWL TORE ME FROM MY SLEEP. BUT I QUICKLY realized I'd been the one making that sound.

I felt it, *the pull.* My wolf was ready, clambering to get out, sensing the destruction around us. It raged to be set loose, to join in the carnage and end whatever had started this night. It wanted to end the world. Now now now.

"No!" I hissed, trying to contain my beast, falling out of bed in the process. I couldn't believe this was it, that it was time for Ragnarök. I sensed the rampant destruction nearby but couldn't believe the end of the world had come.

From everything the seers had said, we should have had at least a few hundred more years or so.

But I couldn't deny my wolf straining to get out, sensing this impending disaster and needing to be a part of it.

I needed to get myself under control and fast, but the only thing I knew that soothed my beast was Ana.

It was everything I could do just to contain my thrashing beast, which meant I didn't dress or call, I could barely walk. I knew I'd be unable to concentrate on driving in this condition, so instead, I went to the roof of my building and simply leaped out into the night.

It was a strain, forcing myself away from the destruction toward Ana, but I managed to summon my bestial strength to launch myself over the city in bounds toward the woman I needed.

Luckily, the farther I got from the destruction, the better I felt, though the change was miniscule. Still, that made it easier to control my wolf, which thrashed within me as I reached Ana's house.

Ana was there, in the doorway, and she was all I could see.

When I saw her, my wolf's desperation shifted. It still wanted to get out... but now it also wanted to get *in... to her*.

I rushed her, pushing her inside and pinning her against a wall, tearing at her clothes, and trying to consume her with a wolf-possessed kiss.

It took everything I had to gasp out the word, "Talk!"

"Fen?" Ana gasped. That one word was enough to make my wolf pause, but I needed more, I needed—

"Get off her, she's mine!" Something or someone ripped me away from Ana and tossed me across the room.

I smashed into the far wall, easily breaking through the drywall and studs before making a serious dent in the solid bricks between this house and the next.

Through a haze of wolf-clouded vision and stunned stars, I saw Ramsey take my place with Ana, demanding her lips as he ripped off her clothes.

Grey roared as he came from the back room and tackled Ramsey off Ana. My wolf saw an opening and I charged back in, losing control even as Ana had a wild, horrified, confused look on her face.

"Please, stop!" she gasped, and I did, obeying her command, her voice was *everything* to me in that moment.

Except I didn't pause for long. Two words weren't enough, and I only regained enough awareness to notice... there were other people in the room. A young woman who looked a lot like Ana, only with copper-red hair, and a young man in biker's leathers who she was yelling at.

*More!* I begged Ana, but I couldn't speak, my wolf stealing my voice.

"Fen? What's happening?" she said, and that finally calmed my wolf enough for me to speak.

"I don't know. Disaster. Destruction. My wolf thinks it's the end of the world and is desperate to get out, you need to keep talking!"

"O-Oh!" She stammered, still confused which wasn't surprising since two men — me having been one of them — had just barged in and tried to ravish her.

Then a fist slammed into my jaw, and I was flying across the room. I crashed through the wall between the front room and the kitchen, then destroyed the kitchen table and continued, breaking through the wall between the kitchen and the back room. My jaw screamed with pain, and I was stunned for a moment before I staggered to my feet.

Ramsey had Grey pinned against the wall with one hand and was pounding Grey's face with his free fist. He shouted something about how Ana was his and he needed her now, and Grey seemed completely helpless against the raging Egyptian daemon lord.

Had Ramsey been what my wolf was sensing?

The raw chaos blasting off him was already inciting my beast to break free once more.

Ana watched aghast as Ramsey beat Grey, then her eyes slid to meet mine, imploring. Something passed between us then, which I didn't fully understand. It was like I could hear her thoughts just from that look.

*Please, stop him!*

"I'll try, but he's half mad," I hissed.

Something occurred to me then. Did Ramsey need Ana like I did? Did her words — or some other part of her — quell his chaos like she calmed my wolf?

I stalked back through the kitchen to the front room, trying to bolster myself for a serious fight while struggling to keep my beast contained.

"I'm terrified of him," Ana whispered, her words helping me to take control of my wolf and use it without losing myself to it. And I'd need to use all my beast's strength against a raging Ramsey.

"I'll see what I can do," I growled. "But don't forget you have powers of your own."

And with that, I saw something alight in her eyes, some idea or plan.

I leaped at Ramsey and grabbed his shoulder, tearing him away from Grey. Grey fell to the floor, limp and bleeding, his face half caved in and Ana ran to Grey, healing him as I faced down Ramsey.

"She's mine!" Ramsey snarled.

"She's all of ours. I need her too!"

"No one else matters, I need her. The world is falling apart, and I can't stop it with my chaos in tatters. I need *Ana*... Now!"

It sounded like my guess had been right, Ramsey did need Ana like I did.

"Then you can have me!" Ana shouted.

We both looked at her as she rose from a newly healed Grey and stood before us. Her aspect bloomed, raw sexual energy washing over me. It made my wolf want to rut and dominate her.

Ana tore off what remained of her shirt and jacket and quickly slid out of her jeans. "You both need me. So have me. But for fuck's sake, stop fighting!"

# ANAIS

I HOPED TO HELL I KNEW WHAT I WAS DOING.

"Mom?" Eva gasped.

Fuck! I'd forgotten she was here. I'd been a little distracted by my guys showing up, trashing my place, and tearing into each other.

"Take Trent upstairs and talk," I said. "He's a good guy, let him explain things. Mom needs some... alone time."

Eva blinked at me then turned to Trent.

"Leave, or come upstairs," she said, "but I'm only going to yell and throw things at you if you stay." She marched away and Trent — doing his best not to look at me, which I had to commend him for, especially with my aspect blazing forth — followed her.

I turned my gaze to Ramsey, then Fen. "I'm all yours."

The look in their eyes was savage, blazing with primal need. Raw lust radiated off both of them, so pure it must have been painful.

Ramsey tore open his pants, unleashing *the monster,* and strode to me. His raw chaos rolled off him in palpable waves, and I saw the extremity of his desire and knew there'd be no foreplay. The Ramsey I knew was barely there. He wouldn't be lubing me up first.

I surged my aspect down into my pussy so hard I grunted with the force of the sudden excessive arousal searing through my core.

Thankfully, that did the trick and had me loose and wet as Ramsey unceremoniously picked me up by the waist and rammed that immense cock into me.

Even with my arousal piqued, it was still awkward, he was just too massive. But after several vicious thrusts, I began to adapt to his huge erection and the pain turned to a bone-melting pleasure.

Then strong hands caressed my shoulder and the heat of another body pressed against my back as hard as Ramsey was pressing to my front.

"Are you ready for me?" Fen whispered in my ear, his cock sliding over my ass cheeks, sending a thrill rushing through me.

The memory of how he'd pounded into my ass swept through me and I surged my aspect again, readying myself for him.

Luckily Fen had more patience than Ramsey and he took his time probing bit by bit before fully sheathing himself in my ass.

"Oh gods," I moaned as pleasure swept up my body and rolled back my eyes.

Bliss slammed through me in shocking waves. The molten heat in my pussy built and intensified, ready to explode as the two barbaric men drove deep inside me.

Fen was slow, shuddering, as if he were holding back some immense well of passion that might break me if let loose. Ramsey thrust with abandon, lost to primitive urgency, grunting with glazed-over eyes, pouring every ounce of his intense, chaotic longing into me.

If he kept up like this, he'd break me... and a part of me wanted him to.

I wanted to know the true depths of this man's dominant desire.

His first time with me, he hadn't held back and had lost himself to chaos. That sex had shattered my world. Since then, he'd been forceful, but never as lost to his passion as he'd been before.

This time, however, he was simply a beast.

And whether it was my own desire or my aspect reaching out through me, I needed to sate him, needed to feel the full extent of his feral fervor.

Fen swept my hair back over my shoulder, dragging his sharp canines over my neck. I tilted my head to give him access and he bit me. Pain shocked through me before melting into bliss, joining all the other sensations blazing through me.

I shuddered and moaned, losing myself to this intense ecstasy. The guys thrusted again and again, Fen somehow finding a rhythm that worked with Ramsey's frantic pounding, and my desire twisted tighter and blazed stronger, driving me higher and higher.

With a scream, the raging, fiery pleasure shattered, sending lightning bolts of body-shaking ecstasy through me. I came like a monsoon, moaning and gasping, my orgasm so powerful I couldn't breathe, couldn't think, couldn't see anything but the explosions of light behind my lids.

And when Fen reached around and grabbed my breasts, kneading with rough grasps as he began powerful thrusts, I lost my mind entirely.

I was fairly certain I had an out-of-body experience. I looked down at myself as time seemed to slow. My fair skin was flushed crimson, my eyes rolled back, and my mouth open in a silent scream.

Fen was losing control and starting to shift, his wolf emerging, and faint sensations from my body crept into my pleasure. Sharper teeth dug into my shoulder, the hand on my breast growing claws that raked my sensitive flesh, and his other clawed hand reached toward Ramsey.

I felt the wolf's need: a need to be alone with me, and knew it would rip Ramsey to shreds if I didn't stop him.

But I couldn't speak, not with the transcendent tidal wave of pure bliss crashing over me again and again.

Then Ramsey roared, eyes widening, as he let loose his release inside me. The swell of his inhuman cock and the eruption of his hot flood slammed me back into my body and I screamed.

"Fuck yes!" I cried, scrambling to find words with my

bliss-addled brain and not caring if they didn't make sense. "Fuck yes! Hot. Come! Yes, please! Wow! Holy gods! Fuuuucck!"

Fen's beast faded and the arm reaching for Ramsey dropped to my hip to hold me in place as he regained his humanity, refocused on me, and picked up his pace. His other hand, on my breast, came to my chin, turning my head so his hard lips could find mine in an insatiable kiss, drinking his need from my throat, that miracle tongue of his tracing my mouth before he withdrew and grunted.

"Keep talking!" he growled, and he moved to my ear, nibbling and tracing his tongue over it before moving back to my neck.

His thrusts grew frenzied and I fought to find words while Ramsey was still unleashing his heat, like a fire hose, inside me. My aspect blazed, drinking in his orgasmic energy and spiking my own bliss back to heights that seared through my mind.

"Ramsey... You... Oh fuck, yes!" I forced out. "Gods... Are you... with... us? Did... you get... what you..." I had to pause letting out a wordless moaning of aching pleasure. "...need?"

Except as soon as I realized what I was trying to say, I realized having sex with him hadn't worked. His eyes were still glazed over, chaos seething in their midnight blue depths. His release hadn't freed him. But, if that hadn't, then I didn't know what would.

Then Fen came, and I lost all coherent thought as two

wonderous cocks filled me to overflowing. Contractions of wracking pleasure slammed through me and a full-body, world-shattering orgasm filled my entire being and sent me spinning.

My pussy contracted around Ramsey's cock and he grunted. His release redoubled in intensity. The huge man crushed himself to me, his searingly hot skin — over rock-hard muscles — pressed to my aching tits, and that pressure added booster rockets to my already sky-high orgasm.

His lips found mine, hard and needful, his tongue driving into my mouth, and my urgency matched his, my mouth seeking to devour and possess, trying to suck out his very soul.

I wrapped my arms around Ramsey, raking my nails over his back and shoulders. My hands tore at him, carving my visceral bliss into his muscles. One hand came to the side of his jaw, nails sinking into him as I sunk my teeth into his bottom lip. I'd have to heal the man later, but right now, I didn't care.

Ramsey gasped, pulling back from me, blinking. I watched as his chaos faded and the Ramsey I knew returned, except he was huffing so hard from that intense sex — and probably his own heart-thundering release — that he couldn't talk for a long moment.

We both panted heavily, regaining our breath, then, he shuddered and let out a drawn-out, "Fuuuuuuccccck."

After another moment, his gaze finally focused on mine.

"Ana?"

I had to laugh, which sent all manner of pleasant bodily contractions rushing through me and my two guys, making us all moan.

"The one and only," I breathed as Fen, still trembling through his release, clamped his hands to my waist to keep me in place for his prolonged orgasm. "How... is your... wolf?" I gasped back at him.

"Sated," he said, hot breath on my neck.

"And your... chaos?" I asked Ramsey.

"Stilled," he breathed, huffing heavily. "For now."

Part of me wanted to shout: *Thank the gods!* Even as my horny self — who'd never felt anything like what we'd just experienced — wanted more!

As usual, my potent daemon princes took forever to finish. We remained locked together as their cocks pumped their pleasure into me. Then footsteps thumped on the stairs and I looked over to see Donny descending.

*Oh no...!*

"I heard a commotion and..." I don't think he saw all of what was happening — at least I hoped he didn't — before he instantly spun and headed back up. "Sorry, never mind!"

The three of us all let out embarrassed laughs after that. I wasn't sure if I was more embarrassed for myself... or for Donny.

When the three of us finally drew apart — Fen having

to hold me because I couldn't stand — we were all a royal mess.

I couldn't help but stare at Ramsey's cock. Even limp it was still huge. Our mingled releases dripped off it, not to mention down both of our legs. Luckily... the front room had hardwood floors and would be easy to clean up.

"That was... interesting..." I gasped as Fen helped me lean heavily against a wall. Even supported by the wall, my legs were too weak, and I ended up sliding down the wall to sit at its base.

The front door burst open — apparently, it hadn't been locked — and Harmonia charged in.

"What in All-The-Hells is happening in here?" Her gaze swept the room, "I could feel your aspects across town!" She blinked as things seemed to sink in. "Oh..." she whispered, color rising to her cheeks. "I... see."

# SOMEWHERE IN QUEENS

*To the east, the dawn begins to light the horizon. It's been a long journey of stealth and subterfuge to get here, but finally... Anubis has found Nari.*

*The daemon of corpses sits on a mausoleum, laughing triumphantly, and Anubis pulls back, terrified.*

*Nari's power rolls off him in waves so strong Anubis is almost swept away, and he knows if he faces Nari right now there's no chance of winning. Not without help. And while there are other daemons of the dead, no one's close by who could get here in time.*

*But he has to try.*

*Osiris has his hands full trying to contain the millions of dead flooding into Manhattan, and if he doesn't do something now, they could overwhelm the god and devastate the whole city.*

*Except as he gathers the courage to act, Nari shouts,*

*"Come out, little puppy! I know you're there. You've come to stop me." It isn't a question. "Go ahead and try."*

*Anubis steps out from the shadows of the small copse of trees where he's been hiding and into the dimness of pre-dawn.*

*"Nari, you have to stop this madness," he calls, in the vain hope that words alone might reach the reckless daemon.*

*"Madness?" Nari laughs. "Funny you should mention that."*

*He looks down at something on the other side of the mausoleum where he sits and another daemon struts out from behind the structure.*

*Anubis fights to contain his surprise. He hadn't sensed her. Her power must have been hidden by Nari's potency.*

*No... not hidden... joined with.*

*Their powers seem to have merged, strengthening each other.*

*"Melinoe, what are you doing here?" Anubis demands, struggling to keep his tone strong despite the fear rushing through him.*

*The daemon princess of madness would also be enhanced on this of all days. Anubis knows if he couldn't face Nari there's no way he can face her and Nari together.*

*Her yellow skin draws tight over her bony, sickly face as she grins. "I wasn't wanted by my lover, so I found a new one." She looks up at Nari with a lust that mingles with her aspiration for power. "Together Nari and I shall bring nightmares to life in this pitiful world."*

*Anubis doesn't doubt that they can or will.*

*"Please," he begs them. "Stop this. You know your power*

*will dissipate in a day or two and all the gods and daemons will come for you. This is—"*

*"Madness?" It was Melinoe's turn to laugh maniacally. "Yes, it is. Glorious madness!"*

*"Don't you see, little puppy?" Nari hissed. "If we can create enough corpses and enough madness, if we can fill enough human heads with nightmares, then we'll be all they think about. They'll unwittingly worship us. Our power won't diminish. We'll be gods in truth and together my consort and I will be unstoppable!"*

*And the worse thing about that insane rant is the truth in it.*

*"You leave me no choice," Anubis says, striding forward.*

*"As if you ever had a chance," Melinoe says, casually raising a hand.*

*Anubis's mind explodes in chaos and living nightmares. He falls to his knees, then all fours then writhes on the ground with screams which tear at the night.*

*And all the while, Melinoe and Nari cackle with glee.*

*"There's no power on this earth that can stop us!" Nari cries as the day breaks on a city filled with walking nightmares.*

# ANAIS

Harmonia let out a long sigh as she surveyed the scene before her. She softly closed the door behind her and pursed her lips.

"Normally... *this*—" She swirled her hand around to indicate all of us. "—wouldn't be any of my business, but given what I felt earlier, and what I'm still feeling from across town... I get the feeling there is more going on here and that my harmony might be needed." She took a single step into the room but stopped there. "So... if someone wouldn't mind explaining... things... leaving out all the... ah... messy details, that would be great."

"There's something you all need to know, though, perhaps, like Harmonia, you've already felt it," Ramsey said, completely unashamed at his nudity, although I sensed shame and disgust with himself for something else. This was not the proud and resolute Ramsey I knew.

Something had happened to him. "There's an army of the dead swarming into Manhattan."

"The fuck?" The words were out of my mouth before I could stop them.

My mind reeled. An army of the dead? What was happening with the world?

I could handle being a daemon — okay, admittedly, I hadn't handled it well at first — but now there were walking dead?

"Like zombies?" I blurted.

At least I wasn't the only one who seemed stunned. Harmonia and Fen both looked horrified. Good. So, this wasn't something that happened every day for them.

"They're mindless like zombies, but they don't eat brains, they drink blood," Ramsey added.

"Like vampires?" I couldn't help myself. I was just going to keep barfing forth inane questions.

"I call them zompires," Ramsey said evenly. And only then did I notice the many bite marks all over his huge frame. He'd faced them and — unbelievable as it may be — he'd lost. It explained the shame and self-loathing I felt from him. He'd rarely lost a fight in his life.

"Are you going to become one too?" I said with a gasp. One bite was all it took in the shows and movies.

"What? No. Do I look dead?" He didn't. He looked very alive, and very manly, and his cock was so very thick and...

Wow, apparently I *could* think about sex at a time like this.

"If they kill you, you rise again, controlled by whatever force is controlling them," Ramsey explained. "But they have to kill you first. I may not have done as well as I hoped against them, but it would take much more than that to kill me."

"I think I know what — or rather who — is controlling them," Fen said with a heavy sigh. "It's my brother, well... half-brother, Nari."

"That lame daemon of corpses huddled in Calvary Cemetery?" Ramsey scoffed. Then he seemed to hear what he'd just said. "Oh... yeah, I guess that makes sense." Then more seemed to click into place for him as he nodded to himself. "And... it's Samhain today. That's why he's so powerful."

"That would be what I felt on the other side of the city," Harmonia said, voice hushed with horrified awe. "So much disharmony and destruction and—"

"That's what got my wolf going!" Fen broke in, eyes going wide. It seemed this was as much a surprise to him as it was to the rest of us.

Perhaps it was the post-mind-blowing sex-brain haze or just my lack of understanding of all-things-daemon, but I was still mostly clueless.

"Can someone explain it to me?" I asked, sheepishly.

If we were going to continue this conversation, we'd all want to be dressed. So, I tried to rise, but my legs were still watery and weak, making me chuckle. That *had* been an amazing dual fuck-fest. I regretted nothing.

"Yes, I think I need catching up too," Grey said, suddenly at my side, helping me to stand.

He'd been out cold after Ramsey had brutalized him, but with my healing, he looked good as new now.

Harmonia's gaze grew unfocused and her expression pensive.

"I think I'm beginning to understand things," she whispered, then spoke louder. "Nari, daemon of corpses, empowered by Samhain, has raised an army of the dead... of, what did you call them? Zompires? And they're swarming over the city in the east. Ramsey, you tried to face these... ah... zompires, but... they overwhelmed you because your chaos was out of control. Is that right?"

He nodded, and I sensed shame rolling off him. He hadn't been able to control himself... My mind suddenly clicked. That's why he'd come here so out of control, to be with me... because... I helped to calm his chaos...?

Oh!

The realization hit me like a three-foot dildo.

Harmonia caught onto that as well. "So, you came here to quell your chaos by being with Ana." She turned to Fen. "And you... you felt the destruction, which threatened to unleash your beast, but you also came here to tame your wolf... with Ana."

Fen nodded.

"And... judging by the looks of the place." Harmonia looked around at the smashed walls and broken furniture. "You both arrived and fought each other... But then...?" She looked at me, uncertain.

I filled in the blank. "I... ah... asserted myself and got them both to focus on me, instead of each other. That was after Ramsey had nearly killed Grey, and I'd had to heal him. Ramsey and Fen then... ah... well, I think you can guess at the next bit."

Harmonia looked at the puddle of effluent around the three of us. "Ah... yeah."

Something else clicked in my mind in that instant. "Fuck! We didn't use a condom." I slammed my fist into the floor. "I swear, Ramsey. If I have your kid, you're taking the little daemon."

Very uncharacteristically, the huge man blushed.

"Ah...yeah," he murmured, palming the back of his neck. "I guess I deserve that. And... ah sorry, I was a little out of control."

"A little?" I scoffed. "You were a fucking freight train, barreling out of the mountains with no brakes when you entered my tunnel."

Ramsey choke-coughed, eyes bulging at that metaphor.

Harmonia did her best to stifle a laugh.

Apparently not wishing to be one-upped, Fen asked, "And what was I?"

Fuck, now I needed to come up with a second tunnel metaphor? "You were... ah..." Oh! I had it. "You were a savage beast, rampaging through the wilderness, charging deep into your den to seek solace and respite. A den that is sort of... between two hills and—"

"We get the point," Harmonia cut me off... thankfully because I'd gone just a bit too far with that metaphor.

Still, Fen was smiling.

"I... think I'm caught up," Grey muttered. "What now?"

"We should get dressed and... I guess we go fight these zompires?" I said.

I didn't really think I'd be the one to go... Except I was a super-powered being now. Shouldn't I be helping humanity if I could?

"No," Harmonia said.

"To which part?" I asked. "Getting dressed or fighting the zompires?"

"Getting dressed," she said, which surprised me. I hadn't thought that was what she'd meant. She looked around at all of us, her gaze stopping on Ramsey. "I can still feel your chaos. It's better than it was, but you're far from containing it, aren't you?"

He grunted with a nod.

Harmonia leveled her gaze on Fen. "And your beast can still feel the destruction, can't it? If you go as you are, you'll lose control too."

Then she turned to Grey. "And you... cousin. How's your void? If you can't control it, you'll have no chance out there."

Grey nodded then seemed to think of something else. "I think Melinoe is gone. I can't feel her anymore."

"Thank heavens," I breathed.

He nodded to that sentiment but then sighed. "How

am I going to get control of my void?" Grey asked. "How are any of us going to get control?"

And slowly all their gazes turned to me.

I finally understood why Harmonia had said not to get dressed. It seemed I had some sexual healing to do.

# ANAIS

Ramsey's phone rang and he quickly found his pants and answered it. The person on the other end did most of the talking with Ramsey only muttering a few monosyllabic words: "Yes" and "No" with a "fuck" or two thrown in for good measure. When he hung up, he sighed heavily, looking around at all of us.

"That was Thoth, messenger god and general know-it-all. It sounds like my uncle, Osiris, is containing the zompires coming into Manhattan, and some other gods are trying to contain them in Queens, but they're stretched thin. They need us to deal with Nari..." He grimaced. "But only if we have control of ourselves and won't make things worse."

"Which means you need to do... whatever it is you're thinking of doing and do it fast," Harmonia said. "My aspect of peace can help out there, so I'm going to go join the fight, but you four need to sort yourselves out — and quickly — before joining us. Got it?"

Sometimes I loved how easily Harmonia laid down the law.

"Got it," I said, even though I had no clue exactly what I was going to do.

Harmonia nodded and left, and we all went down to Grey's room to keep our... activities separated from the rest of my family.

Three of us were naked still, and it was chilly in the basement, though I was the only one shivering. Grey switched on a space heater, and we all stood around for a moment, looking at each other.

"Come on guys, we need to think of something!" I blurted. "Or did you think that just more sex with me would work?" I wasn't opposed to that, but as good as I was, I didn't think I was good enough to magically "fix" all of their broken powers.

"Well, first things first. I'm overdressed," Grey said as he started to take off his clothes.

Fen and Ramsey looked at each other and something passed between them.

"You should be the first with Ana," Fen said to Grey, "since Ramsey and I..."

*...Fucked my brains out upstairs?*

I couldn't help a silly grin.

"Thank you," Grey said evenly.

Wow... my three hot, sexy guys were finally all playing

nice and sharing me. Too bad it had taken an apocalypse to make that happen.

*I liked it better when they were fighting over you,* my horny self said with an overdramatic sigh. *Don't you want to feel them fighting... inside you?*

Nope, definitely not... okay... maybe just a little? What had happened upstairs had been searingly hot, but too much of that might burn a girl up.

*I think it's time for slow and sensual,* I replied to my horny self, then lost all my thoughts entirely as Grey — finally naked — pulled me into a tight embrace and captured my lips with his.

His rock-hard muscles pressed against my soft curves, his rigid cock — already gift-wrapped in a condom — was trapped between us as he drew my moans and gasps into his mouth, drinking his fill of me with a hungry possessive kiss.

His hands moved from my back, where they'd crushed me against him, sliding down my sides. Simmering, seductive heat teased through my body, following where he stroked and settling low in my core as his hands sought my ass.

I moaned as his fingers gripped and kneaded my pliant flesh, building that delicious fire into lava, before digging in and lifting me up.

*Oh, yes,* my horny self purred while I tried to clear my thoughts. The whole point of this was to figure out how to help Grey get his void back.

But he was just so sexy, and he kissed me like he owned me, and that seared all thoughts from my mind.

I wrapped my legs around his narrow waist and locked my arms behind his head, lifting myself high enough so his cock was below me. That put his face in line with my breasts, and with a groan, he buried his face in my cleavage, sucking and kissing with abandon.

I tangled my fingers in his hair and pulled him closer, loving the way he sought to consume my breasts. My breathing turned into short sharp pants and pleasure flooded my senses, the sensual lava growing hotter and hotter.

With my thighs to control my positioning, I teased his cock with my wet folds, once, twice, three times—

*Damn it. Stay focused on what you're doing.*

I shifted my hips out just a bit. I didn't want him inside me. Not yet. Not until his void returned.

Instead, I crushed myself back over him, grinding my clit on his rigid shaft, pinning it between us. As I did, his lips found the pebbled peak of a nipple and he bore down, sucking it into his mouth and slashing with his tongue.

Oh. Oh oh oh.

My eyes rolled back and a soft, shivering orgasm — that only made my desire burn hotter — rolled through me.

Gasping, I rolled my hips up then down and let the tip of his cock play in my growing wetness.

With a groan, Grey wrenched his gaze away from my

breasts and looked up at me. His sable eyes burned with need, but... no void.

"How do we get your void back?" I whispered. "What do you need."

"I need... you," he breathed. "But... my void is a manifestation of my insatiable need to acquire, conquer, and possess."

"Then conquer me," I murmured in his ear.

He barked a single, harsh laugh. "If only. That's the problem. You're already with me, and I don't *want* to conquer you. I want to love you and be loved by you."

Oh... wow. Well, then.

"And you *fill* my void. You're everything I need. I'm sated and don't need anything else with you around."

Yeah, that was definitely going to be a problem.

"But you don't own me," I said. "I'm my own person. You'll never truly conquer me or possess me." My breath hitched as I continued to rock my hips over his tip, taking just a bit more, and a bit more until it graze my g-spot.

"I know and I don't care," he said, his breath picking up. "As long as you're near, it doesn't matter. I don't need to own you... or own anything, just be near you."

Well, crap.

If his void was all about needing to possess... then perhaps the trick for him was to tease him, taunt him, make him want me so much his void demanded me.

Reluctantly, I pushed myself back and jumped out of his arms.

"Fen, go up to my room. There's a large shoebox on

the top shelf of the left side of my closet. Can you get that for me?"

Fen didn't even ask why and took off up the stairs at a run.

"Here's what I think," I said, my voice husky as I slowly backed away from him.

Longing filled Grey's eyes as he watched me get farther and farther away, but I still couldn't see his void.

"I think you need to want me more. I think you need to be teased until you can't stand it. Until your void demands you possess me." I half turned and draped myself over Ramsey. "So, I'm going to let someone else touch me, possess me, and make you watch until you can't stand it anymore."

I pressed my back against Ramsey's chest and leaned against his bulky, muscular frame, never letting my gaze leave Grey's.

Grey's eyes shifted, turning just a little hard as his breathing became heavy.

"That's... cruel," he said, his jaw tensed, and he swallowed as I took one of Ramsey's hands and placed it low on my belly. The other I didn't need to move since Ramsey had already brought that hand to crush against my breast.

"I could get to like this," Ramsey rumbled.

Grey's cock twitched. A new type of fire, one full of jealousy, burned in his dark eyes.

"I hate this, but... you're right. This just might work," he said through clenched teeth. "I already want to claim you from Ramsey and I can feel my aspects rising."

They weren't the only things rising though.

I played up every sexy trick I had: heavily-lidded eyes, heaving breaths to draw attention to my breasts, moans and twitches, and shivering and shifting my body against Ramsey's.

And Ramsey didn't mind adding to my show. His hand on my belly slid down to my slick folds and began stroking my clit and pussy, which meant I didn't have to act super-aroused after that.

Then he lifted that hand away and brought his wet fingers to my lips, and I sucked on them, one by one, tasting my own sweet-as-honey juices. At the same time, Ramsey licked my neck, a long stroke of his tongue from my shoulder up to my ear and over my cheek. The move was so possessive, it made my knees weak.

God, he was playing his part perfectly... although I was certain Ramsey wasn't acting at all.

Fen returned, carrying the large box, and I dragged my thoughts away from how turned on I was.

"Open it," I panted, stretching my arms out in front of me. "Cuff me."

Fen's eyes went just a little wide at the assortment of bondage gear in the box, but he quickly recovered and found a pair of handcuffs then slid them over my wrists.

They were easy-release cuffs since I didn't want to worry about losing a key, but still, I liked how Grey's eyes widened at seeing me restrained. I lifted my arms up and back, looping them around the back of Ramsey's neck to hang off him.

A shiver of pleasure rolled down my body and I locked eyes with Grey.

"Now I'm helpless," I breathed in mock dismay. "Ramsey and Fen can do whatever they want to me and all I can do is... squirm."

"Fuck, Silverlocks," Ramsey hissed softly in my ear, rolling another wave of pleasure down my body. "Much more of that and you'll make me come."

"Tell him that," I whispered in return, aching for a release myself. "Tell him exactly how you'll take me when you do."

Ramsey chuckled. "I love this sadistic streak, Silverlocks." Then he raised his voice, his tone gruff and possessive. "Oh yeah, sweet cheeks. Keep that up and you'll make me spew a load. But since we wouldn't want to waste a precious drop, I'd have to ruin your ass with my monster cock before filling you so full you won't have to eat for a week."

That... was an image.

Quickly catching on to what we were doing, Fen reached into the bondage box and pulled out my leg-spreader. I'd forgotten I'd had that. I'd only remembered the handcuffs, but the box was full of bondage gear that one of my exes had insisted we try.

Fen made eye contact with me, asking permission. I nodded and he knelt and placed the expandable bar between my ankles. The ends had padded cups that slipped around each leg, then a loose — easily escapable — Velcro wrap to keep the legs in place.

Then... he spread the two sides of the bar out slowly.

The harsh pings of the pop-in-place locking mechanisms echoed through the room as Fen stretched my legs open farther and farther, agonizingly slow inch by slow inch.

I was panting and trembling with need when he stopped just before I would have told him was too much. Grinning, Fen leaned forward, sniffing my thighs and licking them before diving in for my pussy.

I'd lost track of Grey for a moment, distracted by Fen, my pleasure rolling through me, hot, needy, and achy. I somehow managed to regain my concentration and heave my gaze back to Grey as Fen's miracle tongue pressed and played in my splash zone.

Ramsey added to the onslaught of sensation and roughly fondled my tits with both hands, making me moan and squirm.

Except Grey's void still hadn't returned.

Damn it. We didn't have a lot of time, and not just because I was about to come. The was a zombie apocalypse happening and I needed to make him *need* me... now!

"You can't have me," I whimpered to Grey. "Unless you take me." After that, I found it harder and harder to speak as Fen and Ramsey whipped me into a frenzy.

Grey's eyes burned, dark fire sparking in his sable

orbs as he watched me succumb to pleasure at the hands of these two men.

"Claim me!" I gasped, begging him, needing him.

And suddenly all the air seemed to be sucked out of the room and Grey's eyes swirled with that all-consuming void.

Yes!

"Get away from her!" Grey roared.

Ramsey unhooked my arms from around him, Fen shifted back, and I was just a bit terrified as Grey stalked in. His body shook with pent-up need. His fiery void stole all breath and thought.

He grabbed my bound arms and shoved them behind his head as his other hand seized my hair. He crushed a possessive, consuming kiss to my lips, that sent me whirling. Heat blazed through me and I was certain I was going to burn up.

How could I need a release so desperately and yet not be falling over the edge?

With a half groan half growl, he stepped between my legs, over the spreader bar, pinned me against a wall, and dove his lips back to my mouth. He plunged his tongue in deep, taking, demanding, possessing me fully.

Then he seized my thighs, jerking them up and locking me in place against the wall. With the spreader bar pressing into his back and my wrists handcuffed behind his head, I could barely move.

"You're mine!" he growled and he drove his cock into me with one hard thrust.

I cried out with an instant, blazing orgasm. The other two had gotten me so worked up that a single hard thrust had sent me over the edge, and now I was gasping and aching for more.

Grey didn't resume his kiss. Instead, he watched me, that soul-sucking gaze consuming me, as he claimed me with fierce, savage thrusts. He pounded in and out, harder, faster, never looking away as if he was trying to brand himself onto my soul.

I mewled and yelped, moaned and gasped, and none of it was faked. The orgasm he'd started with his first thrust just... kept... going. I'd been struck by lightning and it just kept ratcheting through my body. My muscles twitched and contracted, over and over again.

"Mine," he roared.

His cock slammed home, pulsing with his release, and I cried out as I tumbled over the edge, tears streaming from my eyes from the force of my final release.

When I managed to open my eyes again, I was still pinned against the wall, his cock still buried deep within me.

His eyes, still locked with mine, were filled with that voracious, claiming, demanding, possessing void.

Well, that had worked better than I'd hoped.

# ANAIS

Grey had been so vigorous, I needed a moment to rest, and a bit of self-healing, before we could go on. Fen carefully removed the restraints and laid me on Grey's bed as Ramsey rummaged around in the bondage box and muttered to himself about the fun he could have.

Once I'd been released, Grey had staggered to the side, falling to his knees in a corner, holding his head. I wasn't sure what to make of that, but he seemed to recover quickly enough because he stood and came to me, his void still whirling in his eyes.

He sat on the edge of the bed and whispered, "You've brought it back, but now I can't get rid of it at all. I hate what it does to me, hate how it digs a pit in my soul."

Well, that didn't sound good.

"We got it to come back. That's a miracle," I whispered. "We'll work together to make sure you can control it... later."

Because we were still short on time, and *now* it was time for me to somehow heal the souls of my two bestial men.

Grey nodded, jaw tight, and rose to begin dressing.

With a not-so-sexy groan, I rolled to my side on the bed and looked at the other two: tall, blond, and perfect versus huge, dark, and brutish.

"Who's next?" I asked, still a bit breathless. I had no clue how to help either of them, but our time was running out. The city needed my guys and I needed to get them into shape... somehow.

"You'd better go first," Ramsey said, and I was surprised at his graciousness... which lasted all of a second before he continued, "I'd just ruin her for you."

"Thank you," Fen said with an eye roll. Then his gaze swept up over me, his eyes capturing mine, the look penetrating straight to my soul. "Though nothing any man could do would ever ruin her for me."

My heart skipped a beat at the pure and abiding devotion I felt from him: from those words and his persistent gaze.

Fen sat on the edge of the bed, reaching out a hand to softly stroke my arm. "We already know your voice calms my wolf." He sighed and a hint of doubt crept into those aqua-blue eyes. "But... do you really think there's anything you — or we — could do that would keep my wolf tame while I was away from you?"

I had no clue.

Curious, I asked, "What does it feel like, your wolf in general… and when I calm it?"

"Imagine the worst hunger you've ever felt, then multiply that by a thousand. Also, link that to a need to destroy. Only rending the world and consuming it will please my beast."

Well… that was a hell of a lot worse than I'd imagined.

"And my voice somehow overcomes all of that?" I asked, just a bit awed at my power.

"Yes," he said, looking away for a moment. "It's as if the sound of your voice is the sweetest and most filling nectar. My wolf drinks it in and instantly settles, satisfied and calm." His piercing blue-eyed gaze met mine again. "I've never known anyone who could do that. You are… a miracle."

Yeah… Fen had a way with words that made me tingle with delight and want to kiss him and hold him while he whispered his adoration in my ear—

My mind caught on something.

Ears…

*His ear! Yes, that's it!*

"Grey, can you run and find Fen's phone," I whispered, a bit breathless.

"Yes, mistress," Grey said and left.

"What are you planning?" Fen asked with a frown. Then his eyes lit up as he caught up to me. "You're going to record your voice on my phone?"

I smiled. "Yup. You think that will work?"

Fen nodded slowly. "I... think so... and I can listen to it anytime. The question will be whether a recording of your voice works as well as your actual voice."

Grey returned and we set everything up in a flash. "Let's find out." I quickly recorded whatever words came to my mind, which ended up being me going on about how sexy Fen was since he was right there and naked and... yeah.

By the time I was done, I was feeling all hot and bothered once again.

Then Fen listened to the playback and I kept quiet. He smiled and nodded. "Yup that seems to work! Now I just need to find some earbuds."

Two down.

Now I had to solve Ramsey's chaos.

I tried to remind myself of what had helped him return the last two times he'd lost control.

The first time I'd slapped him. Then upstairs... I'd been digging my nails into him when—

And that's when everything clicked into place.

I knew exactly what Ramsey needed.

# ANAIS

It all made sense now. I'd wondered why Ramsey's chaos hadn't drained from him with his release earlier... but now I knew. It wasn't sex with me that eased his chaos... it was *pain*.

Rising, I stood next to the bed. "Ramsey, come here."

He gave me a cocky grin and rose from digging through my bondage box to come and stand before me. His cock was full and throbbing. I'd forgotten how much I'd teased him earlier when I'd been trying to incite Grey's void.

I stepped a bit closer, so his erection press to my stomach, as I brushed his heavy shaft with a single finger. It twitched and swelled even larger, tracing streaks of precum over my belly.

"Unleash your chaos," I told him. "I... have a theory I want to test."

"Are you sure?" he asked, hesitant.

"Pretty sure, you don't need to lose all control, just... let it out a little."

He raised a brow, then nodded.

I felt the swirling discord of his conflict seeping out of him and slapped him as hard as I could across his face.

The chaos vanished.

Yup... there it was. No sex, all pain, and the chaos fled.

"What the...?" Ramsey asked, stunned.

"I know what takes your chaos away, and it's not sex. It's pain... from me." I gave him a wicked grin as I recalled how he'd said he loved my sadistic side earlier. "And I know how we're going to manage your chaos when you go fight those zompires."

"Oh?" I saw his confusion start to lift. With it, I could see his dismay as he realized he wasn't going to get another round of sex with me, but something a lot less pleasurable.

"Yup. You want to play with my bondage gear? Fine, we will. But on you, big boy." I stepped close, trapping his massive cock between us, pressing my tits to his chest. "I'm going to leave my mark on you in a way... you'll never forget," I purred in his ear.

He shuddered and his cock throbbed all the harder.

"You like it rough, right?" I asked.

He quirked a hesitant grin. "Hell, yeah."

"Good." I smiled mischievously as I stepped around him. "Now. Let's see what we have to play with," I said heading for the bondage box.

I had an idea how I'd make the pain last for Ramsey,

but I didn't want the big man to know. So, I whispered what I needed to Grey and he ran upstairs to grab it. Then I rummaged through the bondage box.

Since we didn't have a lot of time, I wouldn't get too complicated. All I really needed was a blindfold, but I pulled out a few other items as well.

First, was a long, squared, hard-leather paddle that I could use to rough him up a little. Second, were the cuffs I'd worn earlier, to keep him from interfering too much. Third, partially because I'd need them, but mostly for fun, I grabbed a pair of nipple-suckers.

Unfortunately, I didn't have any penis toys, since this whole kit had been purchased by a man... for me.

Still, a lot of this could go both ways and I'd see how it worked. The last thing I needed was a small jewelry box. Inside the little box was what had ended my relationship with the guy who'd bought all of this, the thing that had gone too far and I hadn't been willing to try.

"What's that?" Ramsey asked, glowering down at me. I knew he'd wanted to use the stuff in this box on me, but he also knew he couldn't complain. He'd lose his manly-man image if he whined over a bit of pain.

"A surprise." I put the small box aside and motioned to the rest of the items. "Shall we begin?"

Ramsey grunted. Then, oddly, he smiled.

"I like it when you take control," he said as he put on the nipple-suckers. He applied them slowly, eyes rarely leaving mine as he twisted the tubes and his nipples rose, sucked into the containers. His breathing was just a little ragged and his body trembling by the time he finished.

"Pain or pleasure?" I asked.

"Both," he hissed.

"Good," I purred. "But we're not done yet." I put the cuffs on the big man, then slid the blindfold over his eyes and took up the paddle.

"Here are the rules," I whispered, drawing close to him. "Rule number one: you don't get to come until I tell you to."

He nodded.

"Rule number two: until you come... you have no say over what happens to your body. I'm in complete control, and I'll do whatever I like, however pleasurable or painful that might be."

He hesitated, then nodded.

"Good." I whacked his tight ass with the paddle, and he grunted. Oh... this was going to be fun. "Rule three isn't a rule, so much as a warning. I can heal you after this is done, but that only means I'm not going to hold back. Remember, this is for you, to control your chaos. Understood?"

This time he didn't respond right away. When he did, he simply whispered: "Safe word?"

I rose onto my tip-toes behind him to lick his ear and whispered, "Do you trust me?"

"Yes," he breathed.

"Good. Know that however painful something might

feel it's only superficial. I won't leave any lasting damage, and it'll all be healed afterward. But if you really can't handle the pain, break out of the cuffs. They're easy release. I'll stop instantly," I said, even though I knew he wouldn't. The man regularly went to an underground fight club to have the shit beaten out of him.

I slapped his meaty thigh with the paddle... hard, drawing an "oomph" of pain from him.

"Of course, if you do, I'll call you a pathetic little pussy," I added, trying to get his ego involved because this was the only way I could think of for getting his chaos under control. "If you don't want that, then trust me, and let me do my thing."

He nodded.

"Good, let's get started."

While I'd been talking, Grey had returned with the items I'd asked him to get, one of which was a long anal vibrator. It had been one of my recent purchases that I hadn't dared to try yet. It was just a bit too big for me, but Ramsey...?

Grey set the other items aside and began to lube up the vibrator.

"Get on your knees and bend over, Ramsey," I commanded, and he did.

I didn't tell him what I was doing so he flinched when the cold lube found his ass. I played the tip over his puckered hole until he began to open, then savagely shoved the full thing in all the way to its wide base... and flicked it on.

Ramsey gave a long, surprised grunt, and a tremor raced through his body. I slapped his ass with the paddle, and he let out another cry, the sound a mix of pain and pleasure.

"Stand," I commanded him.

He did, but it was slow, his body still trembling violently. His straining erection was going a rather interesting shade of uber-aroused crimson-purple and I traced a light finger up the underside of his rigid shaft, drawing a surge of pre-cum. Then I slid my finger through the slickness and spread it around his massive tip.

"No coming until I tell you," I whispered, before slapping his cock with the paddle.

He moaned and doubled over, gasping for a long moment. I hadn't hit him that hard, but I guessed he was... overly sensitive there.

I slapped him around a bit more, but we were short on time and I wasn't going to draw this out. I just needed to get him ready for the increased pain which I was about to inflict. I felt compelled to give him just a bit of warning. I made him stand, then whispered to him as I stroked his cock, a bit of pre-pain compensation.

"This next part... this is going to hurt," I whispered. "I'm going to mark you with my pain... forever."

His cock twitched and the muscles in his jaw clenched as he fought to just take the pain.

I gave his abs one last, hard strike with the paddle, then put it aside as I went to Grey, who'd been running a safety pin through a lighter flame for a while now. It was glowing red. I knew home piercings could be dangerous... but I could heal Ramsey and remove any infection as well.

This was the only way I could think of for Ramsey to carry my pain with him. I took the needle and went to Ramsey.

"Ready?" I warned him.

He nodded, his body tensing and trembling. I roughly plucked off one of the nipple-suckers, tossed it aside, and grabbed that super-aroused bud.

Then, before I could second guess myself, I quickly slid the red-hot pin through his nipple.

Ramsey flinched but didn't otherwise move, perhaps sensing that any movement might hurt him more. He didn't scream, but let out a long hissing grunt through his clenched teeth.

I removed the pin, pulled out the barbell nipple-ring inside that jewelry box, and quickly had it in Ramsey's nipple. Then I pressed my mouth over the new piercing and traced my tongue over the sensitive area, sending my healing gift into him to cleanse any residual nastiness out of the wound.

Ramsey's rasping groan calmed to ragged, gasping breaths.

When I pulled my mouth away, he shivered, his cock twitching.

"Not yet," I purred. "That was number one. Now... for

number two." And if he thought it was going in his other nipple... he was wrong.

To keep him in suspense while Grey re-heated the pin, I grabbed his monster cock and knelt, taking him in my mouth. I licked off the accumulated pre-come then popped off his tip to remind him.

"No coming until I say so."

He groaned, his breathing turning into short sharp gasps, and I dove over him again, forcing him deep into my throat. I swallowed around his thickness, feeling my throat contract. With no gag reflex — probably a sex daemon thing —I could keep him in my throat for as long as I liked... or at least as long as I could hold my breath.

Quivering hands gently sought the back of my head, combing softly through my hair, and I could feel his tension. He was *so* close to a release, so I pulled off him.

"You've had pleasure. Time for a little more pain," I said as I rose.

Grey handed me the glowing pin again.

I'd wanted to give him a cock piercing at the tip but had decided against it. As much as that might bring him more pain... I also wanted to get something out of this. So, I'd decided on a pubic piercing... at the base of his shaft, on top, where, if we were grinding just right, it could tweak my clit.

But I had to get his cock down to do it. I pushed the heavy shaft lower, then straddled it, feeling it trembling as it grazed my pussy. Then I shoved that needle through the soft flesh at the base of his cock... and watched him squirm.

He let out a low growl, which continued as I slid the barbell in.

I set my fingertips gently on the piercing and infused the area with my healing to cleanse it, then I slipped off his cock and knelt before him.

"This isn't permission, but... are you ready to come?" I asked as I wrapped his massive cock in the comfort of my breasts and pressed my tits around him.

He nodded, and I shifted, moving slowly up and down his shaft, licking his tip when my mouth drew near.

"Can you feel my pain on you?" I began stroking him more vigorously.

Another nod.

"Is your chaos suppressed?"

Another nod.

"Then I think you've earned your reward."

I was giving him a savage tit-fuck and I could feel this cock practically vibrating against me. His entire body was trembling with restraint.

I really wanted to draw this out for him, torture him a bit more, but we didn't have the time.

"Ramsey, my hot and hulking lover, my powerful pain-resistant daemon. When I count to three you can come."

I slipped my mouth over his tip, sucking him hard, lashing him with my tongue, trying to get him to break...

but he wouldn't. He was keening a long, drawn-out grunt, but he resisted my final tease.

I popped off him and let my lips move against his tip, breath hot on him as I whispered, "One... two... *and*... three."

And oh-boy! Did he ever come.

# ANAIS

We quickly cleaned ourselves up, although Grey's bedroom was going to require more than just a quick cleaning. After Ramsey's explosive release, Grey was going to need a whole new bedroom set but not before he hosed down the walls and the floor with a pressure washer.

Heh... pressure washer... yeah... that's what it had felt like.

My mind wouldn't stop replaying Ramsey's powerful eruption.

*You know you liked it.* My horny self sighed.

More precisely, I liked knowing I'd been the cause of my super-hot, supermen's super-powerful orgasms.

I stepped out from my quick shower and found Ramsey, still a mess, covered in his own cum, standing there, grinning.

"You can't touch me until you've cleaned off," I

warned him. I edged around him, his gaze following me. "Go! Clean up!"

"I can feel it," he whispered. That made me pause. "Your pain. I can feel it." His hand went to his nipple then his cock. "I think... that worked. Thank you."

"Even if it didn't, you have fun things to play with later," I told him.

"Yeah," he said with a wicked grin, his cockiness returning. "Later..."

"Yes, later, shower now!" I slipped out of reach as he laughed and stepped into the shower.

"I've brought an assortment of clothes for you," Grey said when I emerged from the bathroom.

He'd laid out several possible outfits across the desk at the far end of his large basement room, and I selected a pair of black, low-rise, hip-hugging jeans, a purple, long-sleeved T-shirt, and my other leather jacket. The nice black one had been torn to shreds by Fen and Ramsey earlier. This one was a dark red bolero-cut. It wouldn't keep my midriff warm, but it looked amazing clinging to my chest.

"What do you think? Am I ready to fight zompires?" I twirled for Grey and Fen who were already cleaned up and ready to go.

"Hel, yeah!" Fen said.

"No, you're not going out there," Grey replied.

Fen and I stared at him.

"We all know you're no warrior," Grey rumbled.

"He's right!" Ramsey yelled from the bathroom.

"I can heal, and I'm sure there are a lot of people out there who might need that. Even you three might need it after a while," I huffed. "I'm not going to lose you or let people suffer, not if I can help."

Truth be told, I was terrified to go. Well... mostly terrified. There was this tiny part of me that really desperately wanted to join the guys and be out there in the fray.

"If we're with her, we can protect her," Fen said stoically. Leave it to my gorgeous Norse demi-god to defend me.

Grey's void swirled in his eyes and seemed to swell and deepen.

"Correct me if I'm wrong," he bit out. "But didn't the Norse Gods mostly keep you out of their fights and wars because they were worried you might accidentally start Ragnarök?"

"Well..."

"Which means you're sorely lacking in actual battle experience. It also means you don't know what it's like in the chaos of battle. We may intend to stay close, but I can almost guarantee that won't happen. And how will you feel if Ana is separated from us and killed by those abominations?"

Fen hedged. "I... I'll... I... fuck!" He growled and turned away.

It didn't matter. "I'm going," I stated evenly.

Grey tried to stare me down and with his void, he was truly fearsome, but I didn't cave. I faced that all-consuming, soul-sucking vacuum in his eyes with my own stalwart determination.

"I'm going," I repeated, my voice firm.

Grey growled. "Fine, but if we tell you to run, you run. If we tell you to stay, you stay. Got it? I can't concentrate on the battle if I'm worrying about your safety."

I nodded.

He accepted that.

Ramsey finished his shower and dressed. Since he didn't have any of his own clothes here, he had to wear Grey's... which didn't quite fit him, stretching over his hulking frame and making him look even bigger than he was.

We went up to the main floor, and I was surprised to find Eva and Trent making out at the bottom of the stairs.

"Did you two make up?" I asked even though the answer seemed obvious.

Eva beamed at me.

"All a misunderstanding," she said lightly. "I couldn't believe he actually came up to my room with me. I told him he could talk, but I was still going to throw stuff at him. And... he did it. He stood there and told me everything as I pelted him with stuff. Luckily most of the hard, nasty things I'd already thrown at you, so I didn't hurt him too much. We're back together again."

She plastered another heavy kiss onto the man's — bruised — face, and it was clear Eva was the one in control of this relationship as she pinned him against the wall.

"Great, I'm going out for a while. You two stay here and stay safe, okay? Is Reia back from her jog?"

"Yeah, she's upstairs with that big dumb mutt. Where're you headed?" Eva asked.

"To fight zompires," Ramsey said before I could stop him.

I glared at him. "She didn't need to know that!"

"Why not? She's a grown woman." He shrugged.

"She's eighteen!"

"Oh... sorry. But last time you scolded me for thinking your other daughter was too young. I can't tell these things!" he shot back.

"I deserve to know," Eva said, taking a hands-on-hips stance, and I sensed a fight brewing. "And if you're going out there, then so am I."

I hadn't been expecting that, and it left me speechless.

She pushed on. "I've seen all the zombie movies. I know what I'm doing: double-tap to the head, that works, right?"

Did it? I had no clue.

"Yeah, it should," Ramsey said. "But where are you going to get a gun?"

Eva laughed and pulled out a pink pistol from her purse. "A girl can't be too prepared, now can she?"

I gaped, dumbfounded. My daughter carried a gun?

"If you're eighteen, then it's illegal for you to carry a handgun in the State of New York," Ramsey piped up.

Sometimes I forgot he was a lawyer.

"Ah... it's his!" Eva pushed it into Trent's hands. "And

here are the extra clips, honey," she whispered as she pulled three extra magazines out of her purse and forced him to take them. He clearly had no clue what to do with the weapon.

"I'll go get my rifle!" Eva said, sounding way too happy about that prospect. Then she practically bounced up the stairs.

"Rifle?" I squeaked.

"If she's eighteen, then that would be legal, yes." Ramsey...was not helping.

When Eva came back down, she looked like some commando from a movie: Black shirt and cargo pants, a backpack slung over one shoulder, and... I didn't know how to describe the gun she was holding...

"Is that a Kel-Tec KSG-25?" Ramsey breathed, clearly surprised. "Yeah, that's still illegal. Shit, woman! How'd you get that?"

"It's amazing what a man will sell you when you come in out of the rain, soaked to the bone in a tight white shirt and no bra."

She wasn't wrong.

"Do you even know how to shoot that thing?" Ramsey asked, still sounding stunned.

"I go to the range three times a week after the gym."

"Fuck me," Ramsey breathed. "I mean, you couldn't ask for a better weapon to fight off the undead. You got the three-inch shells in there or the one-point-six-two?"

Eva grinned. "The mini-shells." She patted the side of the dangerous-looking weapon. "Forty-one shots all loaded and ready to go." She motioned to the backpack. "With more in there."

Ramsey was nodding his approval. Then he looked at me and his proud smile faded. He blinked.

"What?" he asked. "Your daughter knows her stuff and can clearly handle that thing. Any other day I'd confiscate it, but today, she could actually help us."

"No!" I said firmly.

Grey laughed behind me.

I spun on him. "What?"

"I seem to recall another Baker woman being told no recently. How well did that work out?"

I fumed for a long moment, but I knew Grey was right. I'd insisted on coming even though I had no weapon and no clue how to fight. It was clear — though I had no idea why — that Eva did indeed know how to fight, and that she'd probably sneak out even if I tried to keep her here.

"Fine!" I threw up my arms. "Fine. She can come." I turned to Eva. "But you stay with me, no running off on your own. That's the deal, take it or leave it."

"Take it," she said with a giant grin. "Come on Trent. It's time to kill us some zombies!"

Again, she sounded way too happy about that.

Who *was* this girl?

Trent looked stunned and terrified as she dragged him along behind her.

"Technically they're zompires," Ramsey said.

"Oh! Cool, what's that?" Eva asked as we all filed out

of the house. “Some mix between vampires and zombies?”

“Yeah, they drink blood but—” I tuned out the rest, as Ramsey and Eva fangirled over guns and the undead.

This was my life now.

Grey led us to the intersection at the end of my street, where a helicopter was waiting, blocking traffic. And that’s when it hit me. We were going to fight... monsters. I’d insisted on coming along, but suddenly I was second-guessing that choice.

What the fuck had I gotten myself into?

# FEN

"They're not very bright, are they?" Eva almost sounded disappointed.

There wasn't a hint of fear in her voice as she peered out the helicopter window, watching the swarming mass of undead flowing through the streets below us.

It wasn't the zompires I feared, as much as the potential of losing control of my beast. My wolf was contained for now and I had Ana's recorded voice whispering through my earbuds so I could still hear what others were saying.

Except even with that, the world-ender within me felt the pull of destruction, the death, and carnage below.

As much as it was quelled... it wasn't entirely quiet. If anything happened to these earbuds, I didn't know if I'd be able to stop myself from turning, so I tried to focus on other things for the moment.

Eva's comment had been in regard to how the

zompires seemed to be mostly avoiding the buildings around them. They swarmed down the streets and overran anyone they encountered, but those who remained inside might just survive this.

"They're mindless," Ramsey said softly, his voice holding just a hint of fear, which was odd for the large man.

But then, he'd already faced these creatures once and been overwhelmed. I couldn't imagine that.

"They do the bidding of the one who controls them," Ramsey continued, "and it looks like Nari is sending most of them into Manhattan."

Which was what we'd seen as we'd flown over the city.

The morning's new light had shown the swarm spreading into Manhattan, still clogging the Queensboro Bridge and spewing out from the midtown tunnel. There were so many of them, it was hard to fathom the numbers, a sea of seething corpses. Although for the most part, the zompires seemed to be stopped or stalled.

I guessed that was the work of Osiris, along with other gods and daemons, keeping the creatures mostly contained. But there were gaps in the defense and areas where the undead were trickling through. And it was worse in Queens. I could see the undead mass spreading out through the borough.

Our plan was simple: the helicopter would drop us off near Calvary Cemetery so we could sneak in and strike at

Nari directly. If we took care of him, the hope was that the zompires would falter. Though, in truth, we didn't know.

As much as we suspected he was controlling them, none of us really knew what would happen when he stopped doing so. Would they all collapse… or remain animated but uncontrolled?

"This is crazy," Trent whispered. The poor man was clearly terrified and out of his depth. I didn't know why Eva wasn't. But then… given what I sensed from her, I was beginning to think I knew what her burgeoning aspect might be: war.

"Look, there!" Ana called and pointed. We were descending, coming in toward Calvary Cemetery, and she'd spotted someone on the roof of a large building trying to flag us down.

"Is that a church?" Eva asked. Whatever the building was, the zompires seemed to be avoiding it, like they did with most others.

"Whatever it is, it's got a parking lot we can land in, and it's close enough to the cemetery that we can head out from there," Grey said, his assessment completely analytical, as always.

"They need help," Ana insisted.

Grey, Ramsey, and I shared a look. This would work well for us. If Ana wanted to stay at this — hopefully — safe place and help these people, then we wouldn't need to worry about her while we went in to face Nari.

"Take us down!" Grey ordered the pilot.

Ramsey slid open the side door and he and Eva began

popping off shots to clear the zompires which were milling about our proposed landing area. I knew Ramsey was a crack shot, but Eva was nearly as good. Even shooting from a moving, swaying helicopter, her shots hit home nearly every time.

I summoned enough of my beast to aid me, becoming my half-wolf form, then leaped down from the helicopter. I landed lightly in the parking lot on canine legs, with claws on my hands and a wolf's head.

It didn't take long for me to finish up the remaining undead, and after, I went to the single access point to the lot and guarded the way in, as the helicopter landed behind me.

Eva and Ramsey were soon nearby, picking off any zompires that got too close, so I shifted back for now — those two had things covered — and went to help Ana and the others.

Several people were running out of the church. "We have wounded inside. Can we use your helicopter to get some people away to a hospital?" said a man in a priest's robe.

Grey nodded. "Get as many as you can on there. I'll tell the pilot to get them to the safest hospital, then return for more."

The priest nodded and ran inside.

"I'll see what I can do to help them!" Ana shouted over the whirling rotors before heading inside.

Trent tagged along, seemingly uncertain where to go and what to do. He shouldn't be here at all, but Eva had insisted he come, saying he'd be safer closer to her and us. There was a certain logic in that.

Grey turned to me. "We'll get the first group loaded safely, leave Ana and the others here, then go in."

I nodded, deferring to him. He was the oldest of us and the one with the aspect of The Hunt. I trusted his judgment.

Tension hung thick around us as the first group of wounded were loaded onto the helicopter. The sporadic cracks of Ramsey's and Eva's rifles came more and more often. We were attracting attention.

But then the helicopter was away and the group of us retreated into the church, hoping the stillness after all of that noise and commotion would keep the zompires away.

Inside, Ramsey switched out the clips on his rifle and Eva reloaded with Trent helping her.

"I thought you said you'd never set foot in a place like this?" I asked Grey, my voice low so no one else could hear me. Being in one of *That God's* churches always felt a little weird for most of us daemons.

Grey gave a harsh laugh, but he was all business. "The helicopter will return, and I've asked to see if they can bring some others, to get these people out of here. We may not be able to save many today, but these few... we can help. It doesn't matter who they worship."

He was right about that. And thinking of helping these people... I sought out Ana, who was tending to a wounded woman lying on a pew.

This was the Ana I loved: kind and caring and giving. She may not be a warrior, but she would do everything she could to help these people. Ana kept glancing around, making sure no one could see as she slowly healed the unconscious woman and I step close to her, blocking the view of a few people who walked by.

"Thank you," Ana whispered to me as she finished up. "I want to help these people, but..."

"I know," I whispered. It was a constant concern of our kind, keeping ourselves hidden.

She embraced me from behind as I kept a wary eye out. "You'll be leaving, won't you?"

I turned in her arms and cupped her face, leaning down to press my lips to hers in a quick desperate kiss.

"Yes," I breathed, my lips brushing over hers. "And you're staying." It wasn't a question, and I hoped she'd take it the right way. "You'll do more good here than with us."

She nodded, and for a moment we simply pressed our foreheads together, faces close, breath hot in this tiny world between us.

"What if you get hurt?" she asked, voice choked up.

"It takes a lot to seriously hurt me. Same with the others."

She nodded, then her lips were pressed against mine with even greater urgency. "Take care," she breathed.

"I will."

After another quick kiss, she broke away. Grey was there, waiting for her.

I let them have a moment and glanced around the church instead. There were several dozen people in here. Most seemed well, but it was clear more than a few had come in off the streets after one calamity or another.

Ramsey stood by the door with Eva and I headed their way.

"We'll be heading out in a moment," I said to him. "Go say goodbye to Ana after Grey's done."

"I'm coming with you," Eva said, voice heated.

"No," Ramsey and I said as one.

Eva glared at us.

"You're needed here little warrior," Ramsey said. "With us gone, you'll need to protect your mother and the rest of these folks. That's just as important as what we're going to do. If we're not worrying about your mother, we can focus on the bastard behind all of this."

I nodded along, Ramsey clearly knowing the right words to reach Eva.

The young woman sighed. "Fine, but I get dibs on the next apocalypse," she huffed.

"Done." I chuckled as Ramsey headed toward Ana.

Eva looked up at me. "So, you're some sort of werewolf?" she asked. "I saw you shift. That was so cool."

"No, not a werewolf. My true form is a wolf that's over a hundred feet tall and who's destined to devour the world someday." Given how unrattled she'd been by everything, I figured it couldn't hurt to tell her the truth.

"Fuck," Eva said, eyes wide. "That's rough. Not... not today though, right?"

*I hope not.* "No."

Her brow furrowed. "So… why don't you wolf-out and just maul this Nari guy?"

"It's not that simple. I need to work very hard to keep my wolf contained. If I fully let it out then *it* would be in control and it would start its destiny of devouring the world."

"Oh…"

"Yeah."

"All right. Time to go," Grey said from behind me. "You good to stay here and protect your mother, Eva?"

She nodded.

I turned. Ramsey was still with Ana, trying and failing to pull away from her.

My heart lurched, hoping this wasn't going to be the last time I saw my beloved.

It couldn't be. I wouldn't let it be. I'd do everything in my power to stop Nari and hopefully not lose control.

Then Ramsey tore himself away from Ana and the three of us were on our way, bounding over rooftops and avoiding the zompires as we closed in on our target.

# RAMSEY

It had been pure torture tearing my lips away from Ana's. But I had a daemon to subdue, and she had people to save. So all I could do was savored the feel of that last kiss, so desperate and passionate, as if we could somehow stop the world with the force of our love.

Her last words to me had been, "I… I can't lose you, Ramsey, my beast of a man. Promise me you'll return, and keep the others safe as well?"

It was a promise I knew I might not be able to keep, but still, I'd sworn to her that I'd come back and bring the others with me. Then that sizzling final kiss had burned into my soul and I'd turned away. I hadn't looked back, because if I had, I would have stayed with her. I'd told myself she was safe, then I'd left with Fen and Grey.

Even though we'd parted, I still had a part of her with me. Her marks on me — at my nipple and the base of my cock — still thrilled me with a tinge of pain, doing their job to keep my strife and conflict at bay.

Thankfully the pain worked, ensuring my chaos was there, ready for me to call on when needed, but not threatening to overwhelm me. I'd be able to surge it into my strikes, empower my attacks, or just infuse it into my body and become a literal fighting machine. I couldn't recall any time in my life when I'd felt this in control of my chaos. I could truly unleash all my power and not have it affect those around me. Ana was a genius to have thought of this solution and I'd be forever grateful.

The three of us stopped, perched on the I-278 overlooking the western side of the cemetery. Cars were strewn, abandoned all over the highway, indicating that the zompires must have climbed up onto the road and swept over the commuters.

The fact that there were no bodies here sickened me. It meant everyone had been killed and were now part of the undead army marching on the city. For now, though, things were quiet on the interstate. The green space below us was also calm, dotted with holes of erupted earth where the dead had risen.

We all knew where Nari was. His immense power radiated like a beacon from a lightly forested area around a church toward the southwest side of the cemetery. Grey had been using his aspect of The Hunt to mask our presence so Nari wouldn't sense us like we were sensing him, but still, I didn't know how much we'd gain from the element of surprise.

Grey looked at Fen. "You said he had some sort of underground lair?"

Fen scoffed. "Not a lair... though, I don't really know for certain. It's his home. He likes to be underground, like his charges. But I don't think he's in there at the moment. It doesn't feel like he's below ground to me."

I agreed. He was somewhere among those trees.

"What should we expect?" Grey asked.

Fen sighed. "I honestly don't know. The last few times Nari did this, it was just a bit of fun with a few dozen corpses, scaring the locals. This is far different. I'd say... expect the worst."

"Which means?" I asked. "He's the daemon of corpses, is there anything else he can control? Or are we looking at just a protective detail of undead?"

Fen shrugged. "As powerful as he is right now, I wouldn't be surprised if he's able to sneak a bit of power from other related aspects. He might have control over spirits or some reach into the underworld. I don't know."

That wasn't helpful.

"Then we go in hard, expecting... anything." Grey didn't seem happy, but we didn't have much of a choice. "Let's get this done."

Fen shimmered into his wolf-man form, all claws and fangs, and I summoned my conflict and infused it into my bones, truly embodying The Lord of Strife, ready for a fight.

We all leaped away, able to launch ourselves high and far over the cemetery, and landed in front of the chapel only to find Nari casually leaning against one of the nearby trees.

He flinched when he saw us, but recovered quickly, a vicious smile contorting his features. He didn't look like much: ashen skin drawn over a skeletal frame and messy, limp black hair. But his eyes, a sickly yellow, radiated with the power he now possessed.

"Stop this Nari, or face the consequences!" Grey shouted.

"Hello *brother*," Nari hissed at Fen. "I see you brought friends! Good. I can truly test my power."

And before we could charge in, he snapped his fingers. Nari instantly grew into a giant, towering dozens of feet over us, and three ice giants materialized around us, surrounding our little group.

No... not ice giants... at least not living ones. He'd summoned the corpses of ice giants, well preserved, but still dead with hollows for eyes. They'd be even harder to fight. A living ice giant would feel pain and had vulnerabilities one could exploit, but a dead one would keep fighting until ripped apart entirely.

"Fuck," I hissed even as the ice giants attacked, forcing Fen, Grey, and I to scatter.

"I'll take the giants, you two focus on Nari!" Grey shouted as he unleashed his void, which tore at one of the giants, ripping away dead flesh and bone.

Fen grew to match his brother's size a wolf-man over a hundred feet tall, something I couldn't do, but I had other tricks up my sleeve.

I became a storm of fists and fury and I had a nice, soft target in front of me: Nari's foot.

I hammered my fist down on his big toe. I might have been the size of a bug compared to him, but I still hit like a freight train, and my strike shattered his toenail and drove it into the meat of his toe.

Nari howled in pain and Fen launched a furious attack with his claws. But Nari had enough sense to shift his giant foot and stomp on me.

I couldn't get out of the way fast enough... but I'd also been expecting this. I surged my chaos out to protect me, slapping my chest as I did, and the spike of pain from Ana's new piercing kept me in control.

Nari's foot pushed me down and pressed me into the earth. My muscles strained and my bones shook, but my strife protected me. I'd feel a whole-body ache tomorrow, but I was still in fighting shape. And pressed down as I was, I punched a rapid series of blows into the bottom of Nari's foot and his blood poured down onto me, tepid and sluggish like the newly dead.

I gagged on the flow of ichor, but then Nari stepped away, freeing me. He and Fen were grappling now, shuffling to one side, so I took a moment to regain myself and wipe the corpse-king's blood from my face.

Then I was up and launching myself at him again. My incredible leap propelled me upward to knee height. I hoped to shatter his kneecap, but he shifted at the last moment, and I only caught the edge of his joint. Still, I punched hard and the bone shattered beneath my fist.

I sunk that hand into him, holding on so I wouldn't fall. Then began making my way up his leg, punching into his flesh and using that as a handhold to keep going.

A massive hand swung down to swat at me, forcing me to choose between getting hit or falling.

I released his leg, but not quite in time, and the tip of one of his giant fingers brushed me. The hit was enough to send me flying head-over-heels until I slammed into the ground, taking out a row of headstones as I plowed a twenty-foot-long trench in the dirt.

That... had hurt.

But my chaos was still strong, and no significant damage had been done. I'd have a lot of bruises tomorrow, but no bones were broken.

I stumbled to my feet, watching Fen and Nari for a moment. They seemed evenly matched... no... not quite. Fen was losing. He had to keep his beast in check, keep control, while Nari was super-powered and going all out. Fen was bleeding from several hits, but still attacking with all his ferocious might.

Time to—

Grey's scream of pain tore through my thoughts.

I looked over to see how he was doing. One of the ice giants was down, torn to shreds, another was looking rough, missing one arm, but otherwise still going. The third giant had Grey clasped in its fist, crushing the daemon prince.

"Fuck," I hissed.

I gathered as much chaos as I dared and pushed it

into one fist. I slapped my nipple piercing with my other hand, using that spike of pain to push even more power into my fist without losing control. Then I punched the air, unleashing my aspect, aiming for that ice giant.

The air between us shimmered as my shot of chaos rippled out to strike the massive corpse. It hit true, smashing through the thing's arm and chest, knocking the monstrosity back and causing it to release Grey.

The Lord of Conquest fell, landing on his feet, and with a quick look over at me, he nodded his thanks, then was back in the fray.

I returned my attention to Fen and Nari.

"Enough," I muttered. "Time to end this." I'd been able to summon more than my usual level of power a moment ago to help Grey. Perhaps Ana's pain therapy had done the trick. I surged my aspect to its fullest, feeling the roiling tumult of chaos around me. It was nearly too much, and I almost lost control for a moment before I slapped my chest again. The spike of pain helped... but only gave me a moment of clarity in the cloud of discord filling me.

That moment was all I needed and I launched a blast of raw strife at Nari.

The roiling mass struck him low on the right side of his chest and side, hollowing out a hole and tearing away flesh and bone.

Nari screamed and instantly shrunk, probably to conserve power.

I laughed. "Take that, bastard."

*That's what you get for taking on the Lord of Strife!*

Fen shrunk, also not looking well and probably needing to conserve energy.

I'd used up a lot of power with that blast, but it had been worth it. We had Nari now. He was strong, but the three of us were stronger.

And that's when Melinoe struck.

# GREY

As much as I didn't want to admit it, I was struggling. Three ice giants — alive or dead — shouldn't have been a problem for me. But I was guessing Nari's power was reinforcing these beasts, making them that much tougher to beat.

I hated that Ramsey had saved me a moment ago. Physically, I was strong, stronger than any human by far. But Ramsey was stronger, and these ice giants were even stronger still. I wouldn't have been able to free myself from the giant's grip before I'd been crushed. My void was persistent and powerful, but not always fast, especially against creatures as tough as these. Ramsey had truly saved my life.

And that sour taste in my mouth drove me to extreme measures. I couldn't hold back any longer. I'd rarely fully unleashed my void. When I did, not only did it ravage everything around me, but it ripped at my soul and body as well.

But I needed to end this now.

I screamed, keeping a vision of Ana in my mind, letting that temper me, anchor me, as I tore my void open on the giant which Ramsey had knocked down. My void didn't so much consume as it sucked in, tore apart, and crushed, more like a black hole.

The downed ice giant's dead flesh tore away, bones cracked and were shredded as they were drawn to me.

Then, struggling not to be crushed by my own exceptional power, I turned my void on the last giant and did the same. And once it was torn apart, I clamped down on my void, returning it to its baseline level, simmering within me.

Except pulling it back took more out of me than unleashing it, leaving me huffing and sweating with the strain.

I'd done it.

I'd controlled my void.

I turned to the others as Nari shrank, his power waning.

But then a ferocious blast of madness slammed into my mind.

I reeled, but only for an instant. My void consumed the madness and freed me.

It took me a moment to realize what that attack meant: Melinoe was here... and working with Nari.

"Fuck," I hissed.

This wasn't good at all. Even with my void back, on this day of all days, Melinoe might still be a match for me. And with Nari also enhanced... Suddenly I wasn't so sure we three daemon princes would be able to take the two other super-charged daemons.

I did a quick survey. Nari was down, but Fen looked to be hurting and Ramsey looked weak. I myself was far from my limit, but I was also far from being fresh and ready to take on my sister.

"We need to get out of here!" I shouted. "Melinoe—"

Fen groaned, his face contorted in pain as his wolf shimmered around him, howling and tearing at the Norse daemon, threatening to break free. Ramsey's chaos was trying to erupt from him in the same way, surging in flares that blasted up earth and destroyed the tombstones around him with ease.

I needed to get the two of them out of here, away from Melinoe.

Now.

But before I could reach them, Fen's wolf tore out and raged to life in full fury.

I stopped dead.

I'd never actually seen Fen's beast in all its horror before. And though it was roughly shaped like a wolf, the beast was far more savage and sinister looking.

Over a hundred feet tall at the shoulders, Fenris's body was covered in patches of tangled fur, other spots bare, leathery skin exposed. His hindquarters were smaller, lean, and emaciated, but those legs were still powerful. His front shoulders and head were disproportionately large and powerful. His claws were the length of a car, easily tearing up the earth.

The beast's jaw was too long, too wide, almost like a crocodile, and filled with huge yellowed teeth. Fenris roared... and the earth shook. Then with the next opening of that maw, whole neighborhoods were devoured, sucked in almost instantly.

"Fuck me," I whispered in awe.

And with Fen adding so much destruction and chaos into the mix... Ramsey lost it too. Discord and conflict swirled around the Lord of Strife, tearing up everything in his path.

I wouldn't be able to do much now, not as I was. I needed to fall back and regroup... even if it was only me regrouping.

I swore again as I was forced to flee. The bitter sting of failure sunk its claws into me as I bounded away and heard the combined laughs of Nari and Melinoe behind me.

"I'll be back," I hissed through clenched teeth.

For now, I'd retreat to the church where Ana and the others were holed up.

Except even before I got there, I could see the throng of undead crawling over the place, breaking windows and swarming through already broken doors. The building was completely overrun.

# ANAIS

For a while, things had been fine.

Grey's helicopter had returned, bringing a surprise with it: Harmonia. She'd been at the hospital when it had arrived with the wounded. Apparently, she'd helped some others escape the undead and had escorted them to that hospital. When she'd seen the helicopter, she'd known it was Grey's and had hitched a ride back to us.

The helicopter had then taken the rest of those who were seriously injured away, leaving a small group of able-bodied people waiting in the church to get out on the next pass.

But not long after that, things escalated quickly. The zompires were no longer ignoring this building, but swarming toward it.

"It must be us," Harmonia said, dismay thick in her voice. "We've doomed these innocent people."

The doors of the church bulged inward with the force of the horde of zompires pressing against them.

"Us?" I asked, confused.

"Daemons. The zompires must be attracted to us for some reason."

"Fu—" I remembered I was in a church, "—dge!"

"Fudge indeed," Harmonia said, clipped. "Ana, get everyone to the basement. That will keep them safe a little longer, especially if the zompires are after us. I may be able to slow them with my harmony. Eva, get your gun. We're about to need it."

Eva grinned like a maniac as she snatched up her rifle. The sight of my daughter with such a weapon still boggled me.

All of this was too much.

My thoughts stuttered. I stood there, stunned, for a long moment.

"Ana?" Harmonia asked, laying a comforting hand on my shoulder. "Come on, girl, snap out of it!"

Her soothing peace swept through me, and my emotions settled, but my mind was still on the fritz.

"Ana?" She stared into my eyes, but it was like she was a thousand miles away. "I could really use confident and courageous Ana right now," she whispered. "You know, the Ana that commands three daemon princes like they're puppies. The Ana that faced down Mammon, an ancient daemon, and overwhelmed him. Can *that* Ana come out to play?"

Something about that wording made me laugh. It was

a harsh, self-deprecating laugh, but still, it broke me out of my haze.

"Confident Ana is confident in a sheath dress, heels, and when faced with hot guys," I told her. "Not horrid monsters."

It was true. In social situations, I could rule the room. But in a warzone, I was less useful.

"Still, can you summon some of that moxie and power? We just might need it to get through this."

"I'll see what I can do." I sniffed. "I mean, I am pretty hot in his outfit, so... maybe?"

"That's the spirit," Harmonia said, giving me one last squeeze before releasing me.

I nodded to her and got to work, calling out to the people in the church and herding them into the basement.

"Stay with them," Harmonia called to me.

"We'll protect you," Eva added.

Yet again, I found one of my daughters acting more like a parent to me. Usually it was Reia, all logical and orderly when I wasn't. Today, it was Eva, protecting me when I should have been the one sheltering her.

I ushered the last of the innocent people into the basement, following them down the stairs into a large room. People huddled close to their families, clearly terrified. I didn't blame them.

Everything was quiet upstairs... until a horrible screeching, breaking crash tore through the silence, making everyone gasp or cry out.

Then came a rapid succession of gunshots: Eva. Those shots seemed to go on for ages but also ended far too soon. And when they stopped, we all held our breath.

My heart thundered with dread and uncertainty, verging on panic. My daughter was up there and so was my closest friend.

Was Eva okay?

Was Harmonia?

Was that the end of it?

It was more likely the end of the bullets, not the monsters. And from the frightened looks of those around me, they were thinking the same thing.

Tension twisted in my stomach, and bile burned my throat.

What if they needed healing?

I had to check. I couldn't just sit down here and cower if they needed me, and as much as I was scared stiff, I had to know what was happening.

I crept back up the stairs and peeked out the doorway.

Just as I did, Eva yelled, "Thanks, and reload this one!"

More shots rang out, but they didn't sound the same as before.

I opened the door a bit more and saw Harmonia with her arms outstretched and I assumed she was doing something to try to calm the zompires. The creatures did seem sluggish, slowly plodding toward Eva and Harmonia.

My daughter backed up — one careful step at a time

— a handgun held in a steady grip. She fired with precision, never missing her target. There was a wild look in her eyes and a grin on her lips.

I'd always known Eva was a hellion, but the viciousness she'd shown today was just a bit too much for me. Trent was behind her, reloading her rifle, but he was nowhere near done when the shots from the handgun turned to clicks; empty.

Still, my commando-clad teen wasn't afraid. She plucked up an axe — I had no clue where she'd found that, probably in some *break in case of fire* box — and charged at the zompires with a war cry.

I'd thought Eva to be the daughter who was the most like me, and she was, in looks, all curves with my silver eyes. And like me, she'd gravitated toward bad boys and started her sexual escapades early, but this new side of her was nothing like me. This dominance and power, this strength and warrior spirit. Where had that come from?

It certainly hadn't come from me. Maybe we weren't as much alike as I'd thought.

Perhaps it was time for me to learn something from her.

I slipped out from the doorway, closing it behind me. Drawing in a long breath, I tried to find my warrior spirit, because if — heaven help us all — the zompires got past Harmonia and Eva, they'd be coming for me next. And if I was with the humans downstairs, I'd only be endangering them. Which meant my place was up here.

But I had no clue what I could do against these

things. I was pretty sure seducing them or healing them wouldn't be helpful.

I slowly crept to where Trent was reloading the rifle. He handed me the small handgun and a box of bullets. I had no clue how to load a gun, but there was no time like the present to learn.

"I'm glad you two were able to reconcile," I said to him as I fumbled with bullets.

We might all die today, but at least Eva would die knowing the truth about the man who loved her.

Except that thought didn't cheer me up as much as I'd hoped.

"Ah... yeah, me too," Trent said, his voice shaky. "She's... like no one I've ever known. So... *hot*!" The way he said that last word, laden with layers of meaning, made me smile.

"Yeah," I agreed. She was hot-blooded, hot-tempered, and too-hot-to-handle. She burned with a bright intensity that was hard to ignore, and equally hard to live with some days. "You sure you're up for that heat?"

With everything going on around us, he actually smiled. It was a slip of a smile, and it didn't last, but I saw his devotion to her.

"I'd rather die in her heat than live in the cold," Trent breathed.

Now *that* was love.

"I don't know how much longer I can keep this up!" Eva yelled. She was a beast, hacking away at the horde, but no matter how many she dropped, more kept coming. She wouldn't last long.

I *needed* to help.

I had to do something, but an overwhelming fear gripped me.

The zompires swarmed in, still slowed by Harmonia's calming influence and Eva's onslaught, but more and more of them slipped in through the door, filling the church and clambering over the pews to surround us.

"Run!" Harmonia gasped, voice strained. "I don't know how much longer I can slow them!"

Trent picked up the rifle and the backpack with extra ammunition and bolted for the raised area at the front of the church. I followed. We sprinted up the few steps, but... there was nowhere to go after that.

I glanced back. Harmonia was faltering, walking backward as fast as she could, looking exhausted. Eva was holding her ground, but that only meant the zompires were quickly surrounding her, and even as I watched, they swarmed over her.

"Eva!" Harmonia and I shouted at the same time.

Harmonia ran forward, blasting her peace at the zompires around Eva specifically. Those ones shifted and fell back, stilled, and it had been just in time. Eva was revealed, blood staining the many tears in her black clothes. Harmonia grabbed the other woman and her face turned red with the extreme effort it took to send out another wave of peace, keeping the fiends at bay as she lugged a limping Eva back toward Trent and me.

That was it.

That was all we had.

We'd given everything... well, *everyone else* had given everything, while I'd stood there like a post.

I caught Eva as Harmonia handed her over to me. Then Harmonia collapsed in exhaustion next to me. "I've got nothing left," she huffed. "I'm so sorry, Ana."

*She* was sorry? At least she'd done something.

Eva was a dead weight in my arms, and my heart squeezed with worry.

"Guess I'm not so much of a hero after all," Eva rasped, her voice hoarse and her face scratched and bruised as she looked up at me, giving a weak smile.

"You're more a hero than I'll ever be," I breathed, holding her close, and doing the only thing I could, healing her.

Eva sighed as her many wounds closed. I hadn't realized how badly she'd been mauled until I'd healed her and felt how much that had drained me.

The zompires, no longer slowed — but not particularly fast to begin with — had filled half the church. They'd reach us soon enough.

"Trent, how's the rifle coming?" Eva asked, breathing hard.

"Half loaded."

"Good enough." She reached out an arm and he handed over the large weapon.

Except I knew we were doomed. It didn't matter how many shots Eva had left. There had to be close to two hundred zompires in here, and they were piling up so high outside they'd begun smashing through the raised windows along the sides of the church. We'd be overrun in no time.

I couldn't let that happen.

"No," I breathed.

And with that word, something inside me broke. A damn crushed under the weight of my inaction and fear and a new feeling, like liquid determination, flooded into me.

Suddenly I was moving toward the monsters.

"What the fuck? Mom?" Eva hissed at me.

But it was finally time for me to stand up and protect my daughter and my friend. I didn't know what I was going to do, but I knew one thing for sure: I'd found my warrior spirit.

# ANAIS

A HEAT, FAR DIFFERENT FROM THE MOLTEN FIRE OF SEXUAL arousal, consumed me. It filled my limbs and strengthened them. It cleared my mind and suddenly dozens of paths and strategies filled my brain. I knew how to deal the most damage to these fiends and how to stop them.

I didn't question any of this. I couldn't. There were no other options left. Instead, I gave myself over to this new and ferocious sensation and charged into battle.

My arms and legs lashed out of their own accord, striking zompires left and right, plowing through the beasts closing in around us. I couldn't allow anyone past me.

But all the tactical knowledge swirling in my head came to the same conclusion... one person wouldn't be enough to handle all of these enemies. I needed allies.

Eva was shooting again, but she'd run out of shots soon enough.

Harmonia was exhausted.

Trent wasn't a fighter.

The inescapable conclusion was, we wouldn't be enough.

We needed more warriors...

I blinked, surprised as a literal knight-in-shining-armor appeared next to me. It was a spectral, glowing figure, armed with a heavy sword and stout shield and it began to fight alongside me, moving of its own will, slashing — its blade apparently real enough — through the foes.

Then another figure appeared nearby, and another, and another.

I backed up slowly as these strange glowing minions filled the gaps and kept the zompires at bay.

"What the fuck?" I breathed. I didn't know how it was possible, but I was fairly certain *I* had manifested these strange entities.

"Ana?" Harmonia asked from behind me as she put her hand on my shoulder.

I knew where she was and how she was positioned even without looking, just from her voice and how she was touching me.

"Oh!" she breathed, sounding surprised.

A nimbus of light surrounded her which was surprising enough. But then I realized she wasn't emanating the light, I was, and I was healing her of her exhaustion.

Harmonia blinked, looking refreshed and revitalized.

"Ah... Mom? You're glowing. Also, who are those knights?" Eva asked as she ran out of ammunition once again. "What's going on?"

"I have no fucking idea," I said.

"I do." Harmonia looked at me meaningfully. "You're a fucking goddess, and you've just come into your power."

Something about that phrasing made me smile: from *sex daemon* to *fucking goddess*. That sounded right to me.

"And one of your aspects is war," Harmonia breathed. "Which explains why Eva has that aspect as well."

"A g-goddess?" I stammered. No way!

"Yup, and keep your attention on those minions of yours, they're starting to waver."

For a moment, I'd doubted myself, not quite believing what Harmonia was saying, and in that time, my knights had faltered, letting several zompires move right through them.

Fuck.

I refocused my resolve to protect my loved ones. That reinforced my minions, ensuring they could keep the zompires at bay. Then I met the small force of undead that had gotten past them, quickly tearing them apart. I was getting a lot of blood on — what was now — my *only* leather jacket, which made me really mad.

"You fuckers messed up my outfit. You'll pay for that!"

I bolted through my minions and into the horde of zompires, releasing the fury building inside me. I slashed and severed and killed, laying about me with... wait—

Where had this sword come from?

I must have manifested that too.

Also, no more blood was getting on my clothes because I was in glowing armor, matching the knights around me.

I could get used to this.

More shining minions appeared as I made room around me.

"No fair, Mom!" I heard behind me. "Why do you get a magical sword and... oh wait! If you can do that then..."

Blazing bolts of fiery energy began picking off zompires.

I risked a glance and saw Eva with her rifle, only it wasn't shooting regular bullets anymore and there was an expression of awed-glee on her face. She was manifesting ammunition just like I'd summoned a weapon.

Like mother like daughter.

I waded into the remaining zompires, reconsidering my thought from earlier. Maybe Eva and I really were a lot alike after all.

# GREY

My void tore at the swelling tidal wave of undead swarming the church. Windows shattered as more of the abominations surged into the building. There would be no way anyone inside could survive that for long.

But... Ana...

The mere thought of Ana in pain broke my mind and tore at my heart. I couldn't contemplate that option.

If she was dead, I'd die as well. If she wasn't in this world, there was no reason for me to be.

But she wasn't dead yet. I could still feel the presence of three daemons inside, one far stronger than the other two. I had no clue who the third presence was... though it felt familiar. And I didn't have time to contemplate it. All I knew was Ana and Eva were alive for the moment.

So, I redoubled my efforts, as exhausted as I was, and unleashed my void on the horde around the church.

Hundreds of zompires were crushed, but there was no end to them as more swarmed from the street toward me.

It was that moment when everything clicked. I hadn't understood why so many of the creatures had come to the church. There'd been so few when we'd arrived. But only humans had been inside then.

They had to be attracted to daemons.

My heart sank even more.

"Ana!"

I unleashed all my agony and heartache into that one word. I had to get to her before it was too late!

With a wordless scream, I let my void tear at the world. The side of the church crumbled, forming a hole the size of a small house, and I leaped up onto the rubble and shouted again as I gaped at the sheer number of undead inside. "Ana!"

"Grey?" she called back to me.

It was impossible to miss her. Ana was fighting her way through the horde, shining like a beacon of hope.

She radiated a soft pulsing light, pure and warm. Strange semi-see-through spectral armor covered her and she held a sword of similar make in one hand and a shield in the other. Her silver hair streamed like a banner behind her. She was the picture of a conquering hero, of power and beauty.

Nearby, Harmonia pushed back the horde, while Eva blasted them with her rifle, shooting celestial bolts.

Harmonia! She was the third — all too familiar — daemon presence I'd felt. I was glad she was here to help.

"Ana?" I gasped.

"Grey!" she cheered. "I'd hug you, but I'm not done cleaning up here. Wanna join me for some undead slaying?"

Where was mild-mannered, terrified-of-danger Ana?

Somehow, she'd been replaced with kick-ass, warrior Ana… something I didn't mind at all.

"Sure." I leaped over to join her inside the church. Landing beside her, I stole a quick kiss on her cheek. "You look good like this."

She looked good period. She was alive and that was *everything*.

Ana blushed at my praise, then we fought, side by side. And as we fought, I tried as best I could to tell her what had happened.

"Melinoe has joined with Nari," I said. My void crushed a score of the foul creatures as we moved toward the door. "She's feeding off his power and he off hers."

Ana hacked through a half-dozen zompires with one swing and their bodies fell, unmoving.

"Together they're nearly unstoppable," I told her.

"Fuck," Ana said, punctuating my update with another giant swing.

"Fen must have lost his earbuds. His beast was unleashed and is tearing up Queens," I continued.

Eva blasted the last of the zompires inside the church while Harmonia kept those swarming over the outside at bay. Fewer and fewer of the things came at us.

"Ramsey lost control of his strife as well. I don't know what happened to him."

We'd cleared out the church and began to move outside.

"I… I needed help and returned here." And as much as I hated to admit it… "I don't know what to do."

Ana was too busy fighting to lay a comforting hand on my shoulder, but I could still feel her essence touch me.

*I'm sure, together, with Harmonia and Eva we can rescue our friends and defeat these daemons.* She spoke into my mind, sounding sure and confident.

And I had to admit, this new Ana was an incredible warrior. Not only was she cutting down zompires as if she'd been wielding a sword her entire life, but she kept splintering her essence to create glowing warriors to help us.

Soon enough, the tide of zompires slowed, then stopped. We stood in the street, which was suddenly quiet, and a cool breeze chilled the sweat on my brow.

I was winded. I'd fought three ice giants, then jumped right into this fight. Ana didn't seem tired at all. In fact, she was radiant and calm and powerful.

And even before I'd caught my breath, she was turning to me. "Take Harmonia and Eva, and scout out Nari and Melinoe. If you feel comfortable with their assistance, engage the enemy. If not, then wait for me."

"And what will you be doing?" I asked.

"I'm gonna go fetch a lost puppy," she said confidently.

I knew she meant Fen, but he was completely out of control, destroying everything around him.

"Ana," I said. "Fen's a world-ender. He's no puppy." But my caution was met with an even wider smile and a nod.

"I know," she whispered, solid determination in her silver eyes. "I'll do what I have to to get my guys back." She stepped in and quickly kissed my cheek. "Don't die."

Then she was striding down the road toward the distant sound of destruction.

*Don't die?* As if she wasn't the one going to face a being that was meant to consume gods.

She *had* changed.

"Is she an angel?" Trent whispered reverently as he and the others joined me.

"No, she's a god," Harmonia corrected him. "Eva, however, *would* be the equivalent of an archangel."

"Oh," Trent said, blinking, confused and in complete awe. Then he turned to Eva and gave a tired smile. "Yeah... she is."

Eva winked at him.

"A god?" I whispered. And that's when all of Ana's changes finally sunk in for me. She *was* a god. She certainly had more than two aspects now. I'd felt the aspect of war strongly within her as well as others I hadn't been able to identify. "A god," I repeated.

But even so... could she truly deal with Fen?

# ANAIS

I WALKED OVER PILES OF CORPSES, HEADING AWAY FROM Calvary Cemetery. I didn't know how many zompires we'd defeated, but it had been a lot.

And I didn't feel tired at all.

My aspect of war was thrumming within me. Unlike my other aspects, which had taken some time to control — or to discover, in the case of my healing — this new aspect had settled in quickly.

For the first few moments of that fight, I'd been terrified, my body had been going through the motions as my mind screamed at how strange this was.

But then, I'd accepted it.

I'd always fought for what was right for my daughters and for me. Usually, before now, I'd fought with words. I hadn't thought I was a violent person, but I could see now a need for violence in some circumstances to save those you love, not to mention to save the innocent. And zompires were completely lifeless, mindless things. They were already dead and it had become easier and easier to cut them down.

There were also other aspects simmering within me just beneath my awareness. I'd felt them bubbling up as I'd fought. Most were still mysteries, but one had become more apparent to me. I had somehow connected with Grey back there, speaking into his mind—

No, I'd spoken into his soul. I'd connected with him through our mutual love, using my aspect of love itself.

I didn't have time to think about that now, but I did find it very curious. It would require some investigation... later.

For now, I needed to stop Fen. Oddly, I wasn't concerned with how I'd stop him. Something told me my newfound aspect of love would help. The problem would be finding him... then getting to him.

I could hear the distant sounds of destruction, but that only gave me a rough direction. Then, as I thought about that, images flashed into my mind.

The first was of a woman riding a lion into battle, the second was a woman shifting into the form of a dove to soar through the skies. I didn't understand where these visions had come from, but I innately knew I could do that. I could summon a lion to ride, or I could turn into a dove.

And, as a dove, I could fly up to get a better vantage point and find Fen, then swoop over to wherever he was.

I smiled. I'd always wanted to be able to fly.

Just like with my aspect of war, a part of me innately knew how to do this new thing. I latched onto the image of a dove and sort of pushed it from my mind into my body.

It happened in an instant, with no pain, almost effortless. I was flying, white wings driving me into the sky.

It seemed today had miracles around every corner.

Was this something all gods could do?

I had no clue. I'd have to talk to Harmonia about this... again later. For now, I just accepted it as a gift and surged into the sky.

Once I was high enough, Fen wasn't hard to spot.

The wolf was indeed massive, tall as a high-rise, bounding through Queens and carving huge swaths of destruction as his massive jaws consumed everything in sight.

*Oh, Fen, no!*

My heart broke for him. My adoring, peaceful daemon was causing so much pain and carnage. I knew he'd hate himself for it and I had to stop him.

I figured the best place to start was to use my newfound love aspect and try to connect with Fen. Talk to him like I had with Grey.

I flew closer, circling high over the raging beast as I focused all my love and affection and desire for this wonderful man. Then I pushed my thoughts out to the savage-looking wolf.

# FEN

I'd never lost control of my wolf before. For hundreds of years, I'd kept it contained, until now. And it was the most horrific experience of my very long life.

It would have been far better if my consciousness had been completely subsumed and hidden away inside the beast, but it wasn't. I was aware of everything my wolf was doing, the catastrophic destruction and death I was wreaking on the city. A rampage which had begun... in madness.

Melinoe had hit me with a wash of madness and nightmares which had shattered my will. I wanted to blame her, but the truth was, if I had been stronger, I might have been able to keep control.

I'd held out as long as I could, focusing on Ana's voice, still playing in my ears. But I'd been writhing, thrashing, trying to shake off Melinoe's nightmares, and I must have dislodged my earbuds.

After that, I'd been lost to madness as all my worst fears had consumed me.

Fear of my father and the many invisible strings he used to control my life for his nefarious designs.

Fear of losing control.

Fear of losing Ana.

That had been the worst of them all. I'd been plunged into a nightmare, holding the dead and bloody body of the woman I loved as I screamed at the heavens. I'd seen her die over and over a thousand times in a second and that had broken me.

My wolf had taken over.

Yet, even my wolf couldn't escape Melinoe's madness and I'd learned what my world-ending beast feared most. I had never wished to know what a world-ender's nightmare might be, but I knew now.

Apparently, there were two things my wolf feared. The first was Vitharr, son of Odin, who, according to the tales, would kill Fenris after Fenris had consumed Odin. The figure loomed large before us with his gleaming sword and we charged him, consuming everything in our path. Then his sword plunged into our heart and his strong hands clasped our all-consuming jaws and tore us asunder.

A horrible, painful death for a horrible beast that had caused so much pain. And yet... there was a second fear that loomed within my beast.

Fenris feared even more what might happen if Vitharr *didn't* kill us. My wolf was driven to destroy and consume and apparently it had considered what would happen if it consumed everything. Once the world was gone, there would be nothing left for it but a gnawing hunger which could never be fulfilled. We'd be left in the void, forever ravenous, with nothing left but the pain of our unending voraciousness.

I'd experienced both of those horrid fates for what seemed like an infinity of madness before I'd slowly begun to regain myself.

But by then it had been too late. I had been a passenger in my wolf, watching as it had continued its unstoppable reign of terror.

I'd tried to rage against my wolf and regain control, but it had been impossible. My beast was unleashed and nothing in this world — except perhaps Vitharr — could stop it.

I'd given myself over to despair and self-loathing, hating myself for not being strong enough, for losing control, and for all the pain I had inflicted on so many innocent people.

And into that well of despondent misery... an angelic voice sought me out.

*Fen?*

I couldn't believe what I was hearing. This had to be a delusion. I was imagining Ana's soft and tender voice.

But then it came again.

*Fen? Can you hear me?*

*Ana?* I sought out the source of this voice, but couldn't find one. *Where are you? Is this really you? How...?*

*Fen! Oh, thank the gods!*

*Where are you?* I repeated. *What is this?* I had to hope it wasn't some delusion brought on by Melinoe's madness.

*Too long to explain. You need to get yourself under control.*

*My beast has fully emerged. I've lost all control. I'm sorry Ana. I've tried, but...*

*Doesn't hearing my voice help?*

That stopped me. Her voice had always calmed my wolf before. Could the dulcet tones of her words stop it now?

I didn't know, but I desperately hoped that might work.

*I... I don't know.* The trouble was... *I'm hearing your voice within my wolf, but I don't think my wolf is hearing it. Whatever this is we're doing, it's not reaching my wolf.* And if that was the case, I didn't want to say the next part, but I knew I had to. *Perhaps if... my wolf hears you... with its own ears?*

But to do that, she'd need to be close, too close. It would devour her.

*Oh!* she said, trepidation in her voice. *I... I guess I'll have to try to talk out loud then?*

*Ana, wait, no. My wolf will devour you. Stay away from me. Stay safe.*

*I can't. I have to help you, and this is the only way. I'll see you soon, my beloved.*

*Beloved?* That had been the first time she'd said it. My heart swelled, feeling a true connection with her in that moment. *I love you too Ana. So much. With all my heart and soul and being. Please be careful!*

I was a bit stunned when she actually laughed at that. *Careful? Is there a careful way to confront a world-ending beast? Don't worry about me Fen, I'll be fine. I've... changed.*

And I believed her too. There was a newfound confidence in her voice, a surety and power that hadn't been there before... unless she'd been taking control during sex. But this wasn't sex. And yet she seemed just as certain now.

My wolf was massive, the size of a city block, so tiny things didn't really register for it. But as I looked out through its eyes, I saw the white flash of wings, the soaring dance of a dove as it came to perch on a building nearby. It was beautiful, white and pure, and I wept for its impending death as the head of my wolf swung toward it.

Then it shifted and became Ana. I was stunned, but my wolf wasn't. What was another tiny person to it? Ana was radiant, sheathed in brilliant armor and exuding a confident power as she raised her voice and called out.

"Fen!" I heard her through my wolf's ears, which meant it heard her too. "Fenris Lokisen! Listen to me you oversized mutt!"

I choked on those words, even as I wondered how she was amplifying her voice to be so clear over the distance between us.

My wolf slowed in its thrashing frolic of destruction, head swinging up to look fully at Ana. A great cracking sound grated through us... the world-ender's jaws clacking shut as it simply listened to Ana.

This... just might work!

"Fenris... Fen... I — oh fuck it — I love you, okay? And I can't live without you. So, you better get ahold of yourself and your wolf this instant!"

She'd actually said it: *she loved me.*

But then it occurred to me that she was staring down my wolf and telling it — and me — that she loved... *us*.

Somehow this amazing woman could love me, all of me, even the horrid, destructive, world-ending part of me.

My wolf drew closer to her cautiously, curious.

"I can't lose you, Fen, I—"

My massive tongue lashed out and licked her, knocking her completely off her feet... and off the edge of the building on which she'd been perched.

My heart lurched.

My beast's heart lurched, which was even more fascinating.

But Ana only fell for a moment before shifting back into a dove and flitting down to land on the street ahead of me, then transformed back.

"That was thoroughly disgusting, Fen," she said brushing gobs of huge-dog slobber off her. "I'd much rather you licked me as a person, in that special way that drives me crazy, if you know what I mean."

I did. I wanted that more than anything.

And my wolf wanted it to. It wanted to be with Ana as

much as I did, and a part of it knew it couldn't do that as it was.

My wolf's massive body began to shrink and shift as my world-ending beast slowly returned control back to me.

Then... I was myself again, lying amidst the rubble on a street, staring up at the sky, a brilliant, beautiful blue sky. But nothing compared to my Ana who was standing over me.

"Hey," she said, smiling down at me, as a heavy drop of slobber fell onto my face. I got the feeling she'd done that on purpose.

"Ugh," I groaned, wiping the goo away as I slowly sat up.

She knelt beside me. "You okay?"

I tried to smile at her, but couldn't. I'd done far too much evil today, and I shook my head. "No."

She reached out, running a hand through my sweat-soaked hair. Her love for me radiated through that touch, and something else which soothed me just a little. She didn't say anything, just nodded. She understood what I'd done and knew there was no easy way to make it right.

I leaned my head into her touch, closing my eyes, and letting her presence comfort the ragged edges of my soul. With her here, I could almost imagine everything would be all right... someday.

"You up for punishing a couple of corrupt daemons?" she asked, her tone was soft and gentle but her intention was steel-clad.

"Yeah," I breathed. That wouldn't make everything right, but it would sure as Hel make me feel better.

Getting up slowly, I looked around. I didn't want to see the destruction I'd wrought, but... I had to.

I had no clue how far I'd fled from the cemetery. It had to have been some distance, because I couldn't see it, only a massive swath of destruction. The fringes of what I'd consumed held half-toppled buildings. The main path — easy enough to follow — was a cleared area with nothing but exposed earth and pipes and gaping holes indicating basements. I'd devoured everything down to several feet below street level.

Bile rose in my throat, but I forced it back down.

"How far?" I asked, barely able to speak.

Ana put her arm around me, and once again I was soothed by her love seeping into me.

"Far enough," she whispered. "It will take us a while to get back unless you can transform into anything other than your wolf?" There was a note of uncertainty in her voice.

I looked down at her and raised a brow. "No, but I did notice your dove form. That's new."

She nodded. "Comes with being a goddess."

I smiled. That wasn't a surprise. I'd always suspected there was far more to Ana than just her two aspects.

"And... so does this... I think," she said, and she put out a hand, seeming uncertain. But a moment later a large lion appeared. "Ah... I thought so!" Looking up at me, she smiled. "Want to take a ride on my pussy?"

"Always," I whispered. Still, I was just a little confused about how she'd summoned the beast. I kept looking from her to it, as she guided me over to the large cat. "I think you're going to have a lot of explaining to do later."

"Later," she agreed as we both climbed onto the beast. She was in front, her hands curled into the lion's mane. I leaned against her, arms around her, as she commanded the beast to run.

And run it did, faster than any horse, sprinting back over the devastation I'd carved through Queens.

I'd have to atone for that later. Right now... it was my brother who needed to atone for his sins.

# GREY

WE'D WAITED AT THE CHURCH ONLY LONG ENOUGH FOR THE rescue helicopters to return and get the innocent humans to safety. Trent had gone with them. That left Harmonia, Eva, and me to scout the duo of daemons in the cemetery.

Once again, I used my skills of The Hunt to cloak myself and my two companions so other daemons wouldn't sense us.

We crept around the periphery of the cemetery, keeping low and using headstones or the occasional trees to stay hidden. Then, once we were on the other side of the two beacons of power, which I could sense easily enough, I followed a line of trees which led from the edge of the cemetery to where they were using the woods as cover, and we inched through bushes until we could see them.

Nari was dancing to some music only he could hear, prancing and balancing on the roof of the church, a huge grin on his sickly-skinned face. Melinoe was summoning creatures of living nightmare from the depths of Hades.

They didn't react to our presence, so I guessed they hadn't sensed us.

Good.

As I scanned the area for any other dangers, I saw Anubis lying, discarded and forgotten, in the open, not far from the church walls.

"They don't seem aware we're here," I whispered. "I know I can't take them both alone, especially with my sister summoning more beasts, but if we can free Anubis and revive him, perhaps he can help us."

Eva shrugged. "I'm new to this, it's your call."

I looked at Harmonia who wore a conflicted grimace.

"We're only meant to scout," she whispered. "If you go out there..."

Yeah, I knew it was a risk.

I *should* wait for Ana...

Gods, I hoped she knew what she was doing going against Fen's beast.

My heart lurched just thinking of her and that massive world-ender. But she was a goddess now and seemingly far more capable than she had been just this morning. I had to trust her.

I peeked back out through the bushes around us.

A distant crash echoed from the south and west, and both Melinoe and Nari looked, but Nari was the one with the advantage of height.

"He's getting close again," Nari said. "Dissuade him,

my dear Nightmare Mistress." His tone was commanding and anger flashed in Melinoe's eyes.

On any other day, she'd be far more powerful than he was. Even today she might be, but she seemed willing to follow his orders for now.

The flash of anger vanished, and she smiled. "As you say, Lord of the Dead."

I had to repress a scoff. Nari was *very* far from being a lord of the dead, having control over only the bodies of the deceased.

Melinoe skipped out of the clearing, leaving her abominations, mostly mindless, hovering and waiting for commands. Now was my chance. She was gone and Nari was still distracted by whatever or whoever had made that noise.

"I'll be back," I hissed to Eva and Harmonia, then I sheathed myself in silence and sprinted to the side of the church.

There, I waited for just a moment, my heart pounding with adrenaline.

Nari didn't react. He hadn't seen me.

Carefully, I slid along the wall of the church, toward Anubis, getting as close as I dared.

Then, with the lightning speed of a trained hunter striking his prey, I raced out, grabbed Anubis, and bolted back into the bushes, my aspect making sure I made no sound.

Again, I waited for several ragged breaths to see if anyone had noticed... but no one and nothing reacted.

I crept slowly back to the other two. "Take him and get out of here. If Ana can revive him, he could be useful. I'll wait here and... hopefully when she and the others arrive, I'll find a moment to strike."

Harmonia nodded.

Eva took Anubis, carrying him easily, and the two of them began to creep back the way we'd come.

I looked back at Nari, who was still peering to the southwest. Then he sighed and resumed his dance again.

Melinoe returned not long after that. "The Lord of Strife has been distracted once again," she said.

Ah. So it had been Ramsey making those noises.

If he was lost to his chaos, he'd be close to mindless and simply creating chaos wherever he wandered. Melinoe must have urged him in a different direction, probably using her nightmares to sneak into his mind and redirect him.

Curious, I began to move in that direction.

If I could subdue Ramsey, then that would be another ally back in the fight. I'd never pitted my void against his chaos before, not when he was truly lost to himself. This... would be an interesting challenge indeed.

# RAMSEY

I'd seen Fen lose control and watched that horrid beast emerge. And when it had, the chaos around me had spiked. Even though I'd known it was coming, I'd been unprepared when it had hit me like a god-powered punch to the gut.

I'd doubled over for an instant from the impact, trying desperately to keep control of myself, but the sheer amount of conflict and chaos radiating off Fen had overwhelmed me, and my chaos had surged.

I'd slapped my chest, feeling the sting of the new piercing. That had granted me a moment of clarity and control, but I'd known it wouldn't be enough. There'd been too much discord around me.

"Fuck," I'd grunted.

I'd desperately tried to remember the stinging slaps of that leather paddle against me, recall the surprising pain of that needle sliding through my flesh and readying me for my new piercings. That had helped, but only for a moment. With every second that Fenris was free, I lost more and more control.

*Fuck it.*

With a bellow of barely controlled wrath, I'd gathered all my chaos and conflict, all my strife and discord, and compressed it within me. I'd given myself over to the chaos, taking my true form: The Lord of Strife, and had just one splinter of a moment, before I lost control, to use this chaos and attack.

I'd blasted my power at Nari, but Melinoe must have sensed my impending attack and pulled him out of the way.

And that was it, my one chance before I lost my mind and any hope of logical thinking. I'd had one shot and I'd blown it.

After that, I'd been too lost to discord to control my actions. I'd reaped chaos around me, tearing up the city.

The Lord of Strife was alive and striding through the streets of Queens.

Only a few times before in history had I lost control like this. I'd walked in power down the streets of Rome during the Visigoth invasion of 410. I'd swallow the strife of Pompei as it had been engulfed in ash. I'd wept bitter tears when the Assyrians had sacked the temples of Thebes during their invasion of what had once been a great empire under my control. The Mongol hordes and the world wars had almost brought out the Lord of Strife, but I'd been much older then and able to restrain my powers.

Now the city I called home was suffering under my chaos. I raged along the border of Queens and Brooklyn taking out streets and houses, industry, and nature.

Every time I managed to wrangle just a hint of control and try to push myself back toward the cemetery, I was rebuffed by Melinoe. Madness and nightmares disoriented me and pushed me away. Even in my purest form, on this day, I was no match for her it seemed.

So, I wept again for the loss of life I caused. Unlike Fen, who would simply devour everything in his path, I tore it up and tossed it around, like a category five hurricane, because true chaos didn't really care if it destroyed or not, it was random and ruthless.

Then something pulled at me.

It was the strangest sensation. I wasn't being dragged or moved, but my chaos was being siphoned off from around me, weakening it.

I pinpointed the source.

There, ahead of me, Grey used his void to drain my chaos away.

Except I was either too powerful or he was greatly weakened because he didn't seem able to take all of it.

More strife and discord bloomed around me as he drew it into him, and the overall effect was a lessening of my impact on the city, but he couldn't stop me.

He stayed with me, doing everything he could to lessen the destruction around me.

I'd just about given up any hope when a divine voice pierced through my cloud of chaos and spoke directly into my soul.

*Ramsey, can you hear me?* Ana's voice. I'd know it anywhere.

*Ana? Yes, I can hear you. Where are you? How are you reaching me?*

*All good questions, which don't really need to be answered right now. I just need to know how to stop your chaos. How can I help you, Ramsey?*

With everything that had happened, I broke down, for just a moment. My love had found me and wished to help. I didn't know how she could, but the simple fact of her reaching me gave me hope.

*I... I don't know, Ana. I need... peace.*

*How about love?* she said softly, and I felt the oddest sensation.

A great presence, like a comforting blanket, settled over me, warm and reassuring, full of devotion and connection. And, as it came to rest on me, it seemed to lift the heaviness of my sorrow and pain and strife.

My chaos weakened and began to break apart. Now Grey's void was taking more than I was generating and I regained a sliver of control.

*Yes, Ana, more of that. It's working!* I called out to her.

*Of course, my love,* she whispered into my soul and another layer of affection and joy soothed me.

My conflict weakened, then faded completely, and I collapsed to the ground.

Strong arms hefted me to my feet from behind. Before me were Ana and Grey. That meant the arms around me must have been... Fen? I had to look back over my shoulder to confirm this, and there he was.

"How...?" I breathed.

"Ana, how else?" Fen answered with a grin, although I did see pain behind that smile.

I turned back to Ana. "You stopped Fen's wolf and my chaos?"

She beamed, and it was only then that I truly noticed her, radiating a warm light, covered in spectral armor, silver hair flying like a flag behind her: the image of the triumphant hero.

"She's a goddess now," Grey said simply. He smiled at her, and I could see not only his dedication and devotion but also his respect and admiration.

A goddess? And then I felt it, her new aspects, billowing within her. One was clear: war. Another was blossoming: love, and there were still others.

"Hell yeah, she is," I breathed.

She stepped in and threw her arms around me, tilting her head back as I lowered my lips to hers for a searing kiss. "It seems you needed love, more than pain," she whispered. "Sorry."

"Never apologize," I breathed. "The pain helped and I had no clue there was any real way to stop my chaos once it was fully unleashed like that. So... you're a miracle any way I see it."

"A miracle who still needs to stop the rest of the

madness claiming our city," she said, as she backed away from me and squared her shoulders in determination. "You in?"

I smiled. I was weak, but I'd always agree to fight beside this woman, no matter what. "I'm in."

"Then let's kick some corpse ass!" Ana spun and began striding away.

"I like her like this," I whispered to Fen.

"You would," he scoffed. "But yeah… so do I."

"I'd follow her anywhere, to Tartarus and back," Grey added.

And that was the moment I knew: we three men were utterly and completely lost to this wonderful woman. No matter what, we'd stay by her side, bound by our love for her and her overflowing love for us.

I no longer cared that I had to share her. At least it was with two peers whom I respected, even if I didn't always like them.

If this was what it took to be with this woman, I was in. All in.

But that was for later. Right now, we had Nari and Melinoe to deal with.

# ANAIS

Creatures of nightmares and the corpses of giants swarmed around us, but I was pumped and ready for a fight. Not only was my war aspect surging, but my love was building a bridge between myself and my guys which connected us.

It was still new and tenuous, but it gave me hope and strength and the will to fight through anything. Sometime — later — I'd have to take a moment and study these new aspects, understand them, but right now, I had bigger concerns.

My army of glowing minions, along with my own shining blade, cut through anything and everything around us. Ramsey used his bare fists to pummel the foes while Grey crushed them with his void and Fen half-shifted and used his claws and teeth to tear at whatever was in our way.

At some point, we were joined by others and Eva

added her radiant blasts while Harmonia added her sweeping peace.

Together, we cut through the line of cannon fodder until we were finally faced with Nari and Melinoe themselves.

This was the first time I'd seen the daemon of corpses with his pallid and jaundiced skin, limp hair, sunken eyes, and tall, skeletal frame. He didn't look like much and a part of me was surprised he'd caused so much trouble.

Nari's eyes went wide when he saw me, my army, and everyone with me. Melinoe's expression turned into one of pure hatred and fury.

She lashed out, surging all her aspects with a palpable wave that crashed against me. Everyone around me moaned and gasped. They clutched their heads, their bodies trembling with the force of Melinoe's attack as they fought to stay in control of themselves and their powers.

My pulse lurched as fear and madness flickered at the edge of my senses, but I wasn't affected. Melinoe threw her head back and howled with laughter, not realizing I was immune to her onslaught.

Praying it would work, I sent a surge of love to my friends and family, overwhelming Melinoe's power. Ramsey and Fen grunted and straightened while Grey sucked in a sharp breath. Harmonia and Eva stayed bent over, their breaths still hard from the force of Melinoe's attack, but they weren't trembling anymore, didn't seem to be in pain, and weren't lost in a nightmare.

Melinoe's laughter choked off as Nari snapped his fingers. Four pale-skinned undead giants appeared in front of us, but before they could react, Ramsey leaped impossibly high and crushed in the skull of one, then another, and Fen attacked the third one. Grey released his void, tearing the fourth one apart, before turning his void on the other three.

I turned my glare to Nari, ready for another attack, but he swallowed hard and inched back a step.

"Enough!" he rasped, his tone filled with bravado despite his body language.

"You surrender?" I called out.

His eyes narrowed and he raised his hands as if he were about to summon something else. Except the fear that had filled his eyes when my guys took out his giants in less than a minute remained.

"Who the fuck are you?" he spat, still pretending to be in control when everyone knew he wasn't.

I was.

"My name doesn't matter, my sword does," I yelled back. "The only scenario where I don't cut you to ribbons is if you end this now and return all the dead to their graves!"

"Fuck me. I don't know where this new Ana came from," Ramsey said from behind me. "But I *like* her!"

Melinoe huffed and blasted more madness at us.

I barely registered it as it slid against my senses and the others only flinched for a moment.

Grey, Eva, and Harmonia — bolstered with my love — turned to deal with her along with the remains of her nightmare creatures, while I stared down Nari.

"What's it going to be?" I raised an eyebrow at him. His gaze darted around, as if he were looking for a way to escape.

*Like hell.*

I was a goddess and I was in control.

Before he could do anything, I leaped forward and pressed my sword tip against his throat.

His eyes flashed wide with fear.

"No, please!" he begged, thankfully coming to the logical conclusion that he was outmatched and I would kill him if I had to. "I'll end this. I promise."

He raised his stick-thin arms in a limp defense, but I kept my sword up, the tip digging into his flesh and drawing a bead of blood.

"Then why don't I see any of those zompires racing back here?" I asked.

"It'll take some time for them to return," Nari hissed.

"You have a minute, or I start cutting off limbs." I didn't want those corpses causing any more damage or destruction. I also didn't want to give him any time to escape, or for Melinoe to come to his aid.

"Fuck, she's nasty," Ramsey breathed.

Nari's grey complexion went bone white. "Yes, of course, I can summon them, but it'll take a moment!"

"One minute," I repeated, easing my sword back a bit and letting the bead of blood roll down his neck.

Nari collapsed into a sitting position, squeezed his eyes shut, and clenched his jaw in concentration.

"I may be able to help with this," said a new voice, and I glanced over my shoulder to see that dark-skinned man I'd met outside Ramsey's suite. What was his name?

"Anubis?"

The tall, lanky man nodded. He looked haggard and weak and leaned heavily on a tree nearby. One eye still on Nari, I went to Anubis, laid a hand on his arm, and refreshed him. He only had a few physical wounds, but he was exhausted and addled, probably a victim of Melinoe's mental attacks.

Anubis stood straighter. "Thank you. I have some domain over corpses, so I'll help them to return."

I nodded to him as he too sat and concentrated. Then, a moment later, the cemetery around us was filled with milling, confused, clearly listless, but still walking corpses.

Nari blinked his eyes open. "They're back and peaceful. Is that good enough?"

I gave him my driest look.

Did he really think having a bunch of zompires roaming around the cemetery was acceptable? Jeez. Barest minimum effort buddy.

"I'll return them to their graves," Anubis said before I could threaten Nari again. "But, Nari, you must give up all control over them. Release them to rest."

Nari looked from me to Anubis. I nodded, indicating that would be the daemon's best course of action — because I sure as hell didn't trust Nari to finish the job.

"Do it," I told him.

Nari sighed, and with that exhalation, all the dead dropped... dead, once again.

*Finally!*

"Now," I spat. "Someone do something with him before I kill him."

Ramsey and Fen rushed around me to restrain Nari, and I stormed over to where the others were fighting Melinoe. They'd managed to take out all of the nightmare monsters, but Melinoe was still strong and she was holding her own against the three of them, neither side able to gain an advantage.

One down. One to go.

Yet she seemed to possess a greater resolve. If I couldn't threaten her, like I had with Nari, I was going to have to subdue her... or kill her.

And given my current mood, with everything she'd put me through over the past weeks, killing was definitely on the table.

"Give up or die." My tone was flat and I meant every word.

The fight paused as everyone waited for her answer.

"And given how much trouble you've caused me and this city," I quickly added, "if you want to stay alive, you'd better make a really good show of submitting."

Melinoe glared at me, hatred clear in her eyes. "You'll never take my brother from me!"

A wall of madness slammed into me. Nightmare images flickered through my mind. Yet it lasted only an instant before being swept away by my resolve.

"Enough!" I leaped forward and hacked off her arm with a flick of my sword.

She screamed and her eyes flashed wide with surprise.

I was kind of surprised too. I couldn't believe I'd cut off her arm. But she'd really pissed me off. I'd given her a chance to surrender and she'd chosen to keep fighting. I could only assume she'd thrown everything she had at me… but I'd somehow shrugged off her attack.

"Last chance," I growled, bringing my sword to her neck.

Melinoe seethed, her breathing short and ragged as she clutched at her wound with her good hand.

"You're not like you were before," she hissed. Her gaze darted over me, searching for a weakness.

I barked a harsh laugh, filled with determination and vicious intent. "No. I'm not."

She gritted her teeth, and I could see in her eyes that our fight had ended before it had even begun. She'd been overpowered and her only options were surrender or death. Hell, the whole fight had been one-sided. My guys might not have been able to take Nari and Melinoe down by themselves, but with me, Eva, and Harmonia in the mix, the two villains hadn't stood a chance.

"I surrender," she spat out.

Yeah, that wasn't good enough.

"Apologize too," I said. "And you'd better mean it."

Somehow, she managed to sneer less when she hissed, "I'm sorry for the trouble I caused you and your family and this city."

One of my new aspects, one I hadn't named yet, surged up. It told me much more would be required from her, and I was about to tell her as much when Grey piped in. He looked ragged from the fight with his half-sister, but still strong.

"I'll talk to our father about keeping her in Hades for a while. A few decades in Tartarus should be enough punishment."

"Tartarus? No, please brother," Melinoe gasped, all hate and smugness vanishing, replaced by fear.

I didn't know what Tartarus was, but if Melinoe didn't like it, it was probably where she should be.

"After everything you've done, you think you deserve leniency?" I asked, raising my sword, making it clear death was still on the table.

Melinoe's eyes widened. "Stop. No. I'll go to Tartarus!" She shied away from me.

"Good," I said with a nasty grin.

"I see I've come too late," a new voice said as a woman magically appeared a step behind Melinoe.

The woman had long, lustrous dark hair and eyes like Grey's, although hers were filled with peace, not a void, and her skin was fair, if perhaps a bit too pale.

"Macaria, finally," Grey said with a heavy sigh. Then he turned to me. "Ana, this is one of my other half-sisters, Macaria, daemon of blessed death and repose."

Yeah… that would have been useful earlier.

"Where were *you*, when all this was happening?" I demanded, unable to stop myself.

There was probably a bit too much accusation in my voice, but a lot of people had died or been hurt in this disaster, and both Fen and Ramsey were filled with guilt about their part in it.

"Apologies, goddess," Macaria said, her voice soft and melodic. "I was in Hades. I got here as fast as I could. I'm sorry for my tardiness, Your Reverence." She bowed to me.

Your Reverence? That was… new.

"Ah… yeah… well… good?" I said. "I'm glad you're here now."

Macaria nodded. "I shall help any souls who were taken this day to a peaceful death and return Melinoe to Hades with me."

"Yes… do that. Thank you."

"Your Reverence?" Grey asked with a sly grin that was just for me as he stepped up beside me.

There was a note of mocking in his tone, but also… an acknowledgment of that title. And when he leaned in to kiss me, it was with the same reverence and worship he'd always shown me.

I pulled him close and held him tight, glad that the horrors of the day had finally come to an end. As our kiss deepened, our aspects swirled around each other, and I remembered how it had felt when I'd first met him, how his aura of power and command had dominated me. Now my power far surpassed his. His void might want to suck me in, but I'd be the one doing the sucking now!

Okay… bad choice of words…

… *or not,* my horny self said with a giggle.

I forgot about the words and the world and everything else, as I sunk into Grey's embrace.

"Get a room," Eva shouted at us.

I ignored her.

# ANAIS

THE CLEAN-UP TOOK MOST OF THE REST OF THE DAY.

I'd assumed the damage was irreparable, but I'd been wrong. Two gods showed up and began setting things back the way they had been. Ptah — an Egyptian daemon of creation and building — reformed structures in a matter of minutes while the Greek daemon Mnemosyne smoothed over people's memories, helping them make sense of the day's events, or forget them entirely.

Grey told me the two of them were a sort-of clean-up team which was called in whenever the feuds of daemons and gods spilled over into the mortal world.

Except not everything could be remade or forgotten.

Most of those who had died were permanently lost. The news told tales of an earthquake, and some buildings were left in ruin to illustrate this. Osiris and Anubis were able to restore a few to life, if their souls were willing and their bodies still intact. But for far too many that wasn't the case. It had been a devastating day.

For most New Yorkers, this would just be some natural disaster, and soon enough, most of them would move on with their lives. Kids went trick-or-treating that evening, smiling and joyful, but I was on the other side of the veil now, the side that would remember what happened here today.

Macaria took Melinoe to Hades — good riddance — and Nari was set to go before a tribunal of gods to decide his punishment. Grey told me his punishment would most likely be a few centuries in one underworld or another, while Ramsey and Fen would be chastised and punished as well, though not as severely, since — for the most part — they had been trying to fight against Nari's minions.

I was very happy they weren't being sent away to some underworld, but still, I felt... unsettled.

Between the devastation of the city and my emergence as a goddess, I was overwhelmed and on edge.

Grey took me home, but when I walked into the front room and saw the destruction my guys had caused that morning... I just couldn't stay there.

Donny suggested we take this opportunity to renovate the brownstone and Grey offered his penthouse as a temporary residence for my whole family.

I was so very grateful.

My family packed up what we needed and by that evening, we'd moved in with Grey. I was surprised to learn Grey's penthouse had a whole other floor to it, below the main floor.

There were enough rooms for all of us and enough space that we wouldn't be running into each other. Grey gave me his room and that night we curled up together. He held me, stroking my hair and whispering his affection until I finally succumbed to exhaustion.

Harmonia stopped by after breakfast the next day and soothed the remaining trauma still clinging to my soul. Except once I was calm, I noticed that she seemed pensive and distracted, which was odd for the usually peaceful daemon.

"I… have a theory," she said, finally breaking the silence between us. "I don't want to say anything yet, I need to do a bit more research. I'll be back for dinner tonight, and hopefully, I'll know more by then and be able to speak with confidence."

"A theory about what?" I asked.

"You'll see," she said cryptically. "It's nothing bad, I promise."

I shrugged, feeling far more at peace now that she'd soothed my worries. I trusted her.

After Harmonia left, I begged for some time alone and bundled up, going out onto Grey's deck.

It was the second day of November, and this high up, a brisk wind made it inhospitable to be outside, but still, I lingered. I sat cross-legged on the deck, with blankets draped around me for warmth, and tried to connect with myself.

After yesterday, I could feel so many more aspects within me and I wanted to try to identify each of them, find out more about it… and myself.

I began with the aspects I already knew. Sex. It was a sultry and stimulating heat that I could move around my body but which mostly sat between my legs. I could summon it and suppress it fairly well now after a month or so of practice.

Healing — or rather health — was newer but still mostly controlled. I felt it as a tingling, mostly on my palms, but also all over me, within and without. With it came a sort-of strange biological *knowing*.

I'd never been good at biology in school, but I now had a sense of rightness and wrongness within my body — or others — and a knowledge of how to manipulate that.

As I sat with my aspect of health, I felt something strange within me. It wasn't a wrongness, but it wasn't truly *me* either. I spent a long time trying to feel through this, but couldn't quite put my finger on what it was. I decided I'd come back to it later. For now, I moved on.

Of my new aspects, the one which had come in the strongest, was war. I trembled when I focused on it, not a pleasant power. It sought to dominate, kill, and destroy. An all-consuming heat seemed to radiate from my entire body — making me sweat under my layers of blankets — strengthening me. It brought a sort of laser-focus to my mind, which saw everything around me as a threat and gave me all sorts of ways to defeat them.

I resisted the urge to suppress the aspect. I needed to feel it, understand it, to control it. I let it seep into my bones — which I hated — then slowly began to rein it in and make it mine, so I could control it. Only then did I let it go.

When it was gone, I felt an overwhelming sense of peace. I sighed heavily, releasing as much tension from my body as I could.

War would be useful if I had to defend myself or those I loved, but otherwise, I wanted nothing to do with it.

Now, on to more pleasant sensations and aspects.

Love had allowed me to communicate and connect with my guys yesterday. I concentrated and the aspect rose up within me. I smiled at its pleasant warmth, which spread through my chest and even up to my cheeks.

It was like… like the warm blankets I'd draped over myself, only within me, comforting me from the inside out.

There was also a sense of external connection. That must have been what I'd used to reach out to my guys. Even now, I felt it seeking out and finding those nearby: Grey, Eva, Reia, even Uncle Donny. I loved them all, and through my aspect, I could feel them.

Compared to war, this was *far* more pleasant to sit with. I learned how it felt and taught myself how to temper it and control it. When I suppressed it, I felt a sort-of sorrow seep into me, a loss, almost like a hang-over. Taking away the high that came with love wasn't pleasant, so I let just a touch of love back into me until that contented warmth returned.

After that, I began to experiment, trying to identify the other aspects simmering within me.

I suspected I had an aspect of fertility. It hadn't come out yesterday, but it would explain why the pill hadn't really worked for me.

I took a long time, seeking within myself, but this one didn't come out easily.

The trouble was, it overlapped with the aspect of sex and seemed to be closely related to the aspect of health, and I had trouble separating it from those others at first.

All three were connected, but they were also different. It took me a while to make the distinction. I began with where I felt them in my body.

Sex was heated and low between my legs. While health was a general sense of well-being, within and without, but also tingling on my palms. Fertility manifested with a warmth, low on my torso, and a sense of fullness across my chest, which made sense.

Once I'd isolated that, I was able to delve a little deeper into fertility and I found a feeling of connectedness, like with love, but this one was internal, the bond between a mother and child.

Wait...?

And suddenly that strangeness I'd felt with my health aspect earlier made sense.

*Oh, fuck...*

Now that I was focusing on it, I could feel it.

I was pregnant.

I sharpened my awareness on this new life within me. Ramsey was the only one who'd been with me without protection, so it had to be his. The first time had been almost a month ago when he'd burst and shredded the condom he'd worn, and the second time had been yesterday when he'd been lost to his chaos.

Still, I was curious which of those two times had led to conception.

I felt through my aspect and discovered the new life was barely there, just a cluster of cells. So, I'd conceived yesterday. I was amazed at my internal awareness and the hyper-accurate assessment of my progress. If only I'd had this twenty years ago!

I sighed.

Some — more intellectual — part of me knew that I could use my aspect of fertility and simply let this extremely new life go, ending things before they got too far along.

But a larger part of me didn't want to do that.

As much as I had no desire to be thirty-eight and pregnant, I wanted to feel this new life grow and see who they'd become. I'd have to find another goddess of fertility and see how I could use this aspect. Perhaps Freyja would be willing to talk? I wouldn't mind being pregnant if I could make the whole experience a bit more pleasant, maybe even... quicker?

For now, I simply held this new life within me and

cherished it. As I did, I took time to learn as much as I could about the aspect of fertility, and how it felt.

It occurred to me — a little late now — that if I had complete control over my fertility... perhaps I could turn it off all together, assuming I didn't want any more kids. An interesting thought.

I'd been out on the deck for a while and morning was wearing away, the sun high in the sky. My stomach rumbled, telling me I should eat something soon — I *was* eating for two now — but I stayed out a bit longer.

There had been another aspect I'd felt yesterday, something vaguely associated with war, but... different. I'd felt a sort of righteousness, a clarity of right and wrong. It had linked to my war insomuch as I'd needed to protect and defend what was right.

I searched within me now and tried to summon that balance, that aura of truth... or whatever it was. Truth wasn't right, but it seemed... close.

My senses slipped over and around this aspect, enough that I was certain there was something there, but I couldn't get a handle on it.

I sighed, as my stomach protested yet again, and gave up for now.

Oddly, as the family gathered for lunch, that new aspect I couldn't identify seemed to connect with Reia. I suspected whatever it was, I'd passed it on to my youngest. Except she was the daughter I understood the least, so perhaps it was appropriate that this aspect was hard for me to recognize and accept. I'd have to talk with her about it, but I saved that for another time. Instead, after lunch, I asked Eva and Trent to join me in the downstairs lounge.

The downstairs of Grey's penthouse was larger than the floor above, stretching out under the deck. The main room was L-shaped with the inside of the "L" being glass walls to see into the swimming pool above. The room itself was large and broken into areas, a lounge with a bar, a games area with a pool table, and even a home gym. Off of this, along the outside of the L-shape, were other bedrooms, a utility room, a laundry room, and so on.

The three of us sat in front of a large gas fireplace, on plush chairs and couches, and they both looked at me expectantly.

"I just wanted to make sure you two were good now?" I asked, seeking out with my love aspect to connect with them and see if love was truly in their hearts. There was a budding warmth there, but it was still new... interesting.

Oddly, it was Trent who spoke first. He'd been deferring to Eva since yesterday as if he were a puppy and she his master.

"I'll be honest, Ms. Baker," he said looking at Eva. She returned the look and they both smiled. "Our relationship before was... ah... a little rocky."

Eva scoffed. "We fucked and we fought. There wasn't much more than that."

Trent cleared his throat. "Ah... yeah."

That explained the relatively new feeling of love between them.

Trent sighed as the two of them continued to gaze into each other's eyes. "But then she left, and I realized that I missed her with all my heart. I missed more than just the... ah... intimacy and arguments. I missed *her*. I missed her silver eyes and red hair. I missed the way she laughed. I missed hearing her breathing when I woke in the middle of the night, and I even missed our fights. I... I was wrong most of the time and she... she was making me a better person."

"Hell yeah, I was." Eva nodded.

"And yesterday, when I learned that she's an angel—"

"Daemon," I corrected him. How long had it been since I was the one being corrected?

"Ah... yeah, right. Well, that was wonderous and terrifying, but also... it made so much sense. She's so powerful and strong and sexy and I... I just can't stand to be without her. I can only hope she feels the same and I'm lucky enough to share my life with her."

I sensed something then. Eva seemed to explode with lust, and it overwhelmed me for a moment, making *me* really horny. I had to breathe through it, finding and controlling my own aspect of sex. By the time I had, Eva was straddling Trent, hips grinding on his lap as she devoured his face with kisses.

Well, *that* explained a lot. I could see quite clearly now that Eva had gotten my aspects of sex and war. What a combo. No wonder she was a handful.

But I knew a thing or two now, and I quickly sapped

the sex from them so we could continue our conversation.

Eva swiveled off Trent, falling onto the couch next to him with a great smile and heaving breaths, while Trent was flushed, wearing a silly grin.

"Eva, it seems you feel the same way for Trent?" I supplied.

"Oh, yeah," she breathed, coming down from her sex-high. She looked at him and they locked eyes again. "He's right. Before what we had was good, but it wasn't...deep. But any man who'd follow me through a day like yesterday. That's the man for me."

"I hope that never happens again," Trent said softly.

Even Eva nodded. "It was pretty intense and scary as fuck, but... I think I'm going to seek out more of that, sorry."

I felt their tenuous love tremble in that moment.

"Oh?" I asked.

Eva looked at me. "I think..." She laughed. "I've never really known what I wanted to do with my life, but I think I do now. I did a little research this morning. I want to enroll in an officer's training program at college. I'll need to finish some high-school courses I missed or get my GED or something, but I want to join the army, or navy, or... something." Trent looked a little dismayed at this. She turned to him. "You can be my house-husband and work on the bases, fixing their trucks or something."

"I really like my little motorcycle shop, though."

Eva nodded. "I know. We'll talk and figure it out." She

leaned in for a quick kiss, then ran a hand through his hair. "Don't you worry, my Fifty-Cal, we'll make it work."

"Fifty-Cal?" I couldn't help but ask. That was an odd nickname.

Eva smiled at me. "Yeah, I've got a thing for guns and a fifty-caliber is one of the largest out there, and... so is Trent's cock. Why do you think I stayed with him so long? Whenever he comes it feels like he's blasting me open down there."

I did *not* need to know that.

Trent gave an I'm-a-manly-man grin. "Is that really what it feels like?"

"Hell, yeah!"

"Oh. I love you, Eva!"

"Love you too, Fifty-Cal."

They kissed for a moment, and their love swelled again. I got the feeling theirs would be a rocky relationship, but I also felt like it would work out.

"Great," I said, and they drew back from each other at my words. "Eva, can I speak to you alone?"

Trent nodded, kissed Eva one last time, then went back upstairs.

"Is this goddess business?" Eva asked.

"Yeah, I wanted to tell you more about your aspects of sex and war and how to control them."

That... took all afternoon, but by dinner, I felt like she had a good grip on things and could develop on her own from there.

Trent had gone out for the afternoon, visiting his

sister, and he'd brought her with him when he'd returned, figuring she'd be safer here, since her abusive husband might be able to track her back to Trent's garage.

Fen and Ramsey joined us for dinner that evening and when Trent spoke about his sister's plight, Ramsey said he'd help her out with all the legalities and make her jerk-of-a-husband pay through the nose when they divorced.

Harmonia was conspicuously absent at dinner, but she sent a text saying she was still confirming her theory and might stop by later.

Which meant I had an evening to myself... with my guys... and after all that had happened, I was *so* going to take advantage of that. So, after dinner had been cleaned up, the four of us went to Grey's room for some... fun.

# ANAIS

I CLOSED THE DOOR BEHIND US AND LEANED AGAINST IT. There was something I needed to address before we began.

"Ramsey, you should know: I'm pregnant. It's yours. I'm going to have it, and you're going to do more than your fair share to raise it. None of these things are up for debate."

He gave a shocked laugh. "Oh... wow... ah... yeah... for you Silverlocks, I'll do whatever you ask, whatever you need."

"Good."

"Something tells me if we're all going to be in this together," Fen said. "Grey and I will be helping out as well."

Grey nodded, mostly stoic, but with a hint of a smile.

Well, that was more than I'd expected. "Gods, I love

you guys! Now, enough talk of babies. You three need to ravish me."

"Since you're already preggers, does that mean no condoms?" Ramsey asked with a grin.

I… guess it did. I *was* already pregnant. I couldn't get *more* pregnant. Well, that wasn't true. I could have… twins. That was a thing that could happen, right?

Huh… That gave me an idea.

"About that…" I looked at Fen and Grey. "Did either of you want kids?" They might already have kids. I knew Fen had a daughter. So, to be clear, I added, "With me?"

Fen gave a wide smile. "I already have a daughter, but… Hel yeah, I'd love to have another child with you."

I looked at Grey. His void spun in his eyes but I could easily resist it now. Slowly he smiled.

"I… didn't have a great father figure, none of us did," he said. "I hadn't thought I'd wanted a child, but with you, Ana… I'd love to share that with you."

"Done!" I summoned my fertility aspect — might as well get all three kids out of the way now – and drew a couple more eggs out from within me. Now I just had to make sure the right sperm got to the right egg. Sure… I could do that.

"Okay… now ravish me!" I switched on my sex aspect and sent it searing into all three of them, as well as myself. Not that they'd needed it. They'd all looked hungry for me before I amped up their sex drive.

The three of them stripped for me, and I let my

arousal build as I watched more and more of their sexy, hulking, muscled skin come into view.

Ramsey, frustrated with his pants, simply ripped them off. The sound of tearing fabric went straight from my ears to my pussy, and I let out a low, breathy moan as my folds flooded.

I pressed my legs together, trying to keep myself contained, but... soon enough all three guys were naked before me and that was getting harder and harder.

Grey's olive-tanned skin glistened over taut muscles. Tall and broad, with that ideal V from his shoulders down to his narrow waist, he was the picture of manly perfection.

Ramsey's muscles bunched and twitched on his hulking frame. Those heavy, rolling hills heaped on shoulders, chest, arms, and legs almost seemed impossible. His midnight blue eyes were already undressing me, his monster cock thick and towering.

Fen was pale perfection: tall and lean but hiding immense strength in those sleek muscles. The aqua-blue pools of his eyes were so calm I felt like I could dive right into them.

They all came to me, slowly surrounding me, pulling me away from the door to crush in on all sides. For once they weren't arguing over me. They didn't care the others were there. They wanted me equally.

I whimpered at the thought of all three possessing me at once. Heat captured me, blossoming out from my core to sizzle through my veins and flush my skin. My face —

my entire body — grew searing hot as I leaned back against Grey and their hands began to roam over me.

I wasn't sure if it needed saying, but I figured I'd make it clear. "I want all of you... at once," I breathed.

Ramsey gave a grunt of acceptance.

Fen whispered, "Yes, of course."

"Anything for my goddess," Grey said with reverence. I shivered at his hot breath on my ear. Then he was kissing my hair and neck and shoulders over my shirt.

Ramsey captured my lips and stole my breath in a devouring kiss, we opened instantly, our tongues dueling with hungry, aching need.

Fen knelt before me and pulled down the side zipper on my flirty, casual, calf-length, pleated skirt. But he didn't let it slip down, he caught it, and instead kissed the small patch of exposed skin at the zipper.

Grey was also keeping the skirt from falling off with one of his hands clamped to my butt, massaging that cheek in wonderful ways.

Not to be outdone, Ramsey grabbed my breast, his incredibly strong fingers digging in and kneading the already sensitive orb. Even through my shirt and bra, I felt his heavy press and my nipple responded with urgency, surging to a taut peak.

"More," I breathed when Ramsey finally left my lips.

The raging bonfire in Ramsey's eyes made me weak in the knees. He didn't say anything, but I sensed his thought, perhaps through our love connection?

"Do it," I told him.

He grabbed the collar of my T-shirt and tore it open down the front. And like with his pants, the ripping sound sent searing bliss to every part of my being, shocking through me like lightning. I gasped and whimpered as the throbbing, pulsing need in my core surged with liquid heat. Ramsey popped open my front-clasping bra and my breasts seemed to explode out of the restraining fabric. Then he dipped down and took one nipple in his mouth, sucking and licking, while crushing his hand against the other.

And with Grey whispering soft, heated words of love in my ear, between kisses on my neck and cheek, and Fen slowly opening my skirt and tracing kisses down my flesh, inching closer and closer to my core… I couldn't hold it any longer.

"Fen! Now!" I gasped and hoped he understood.

He did, letting my skirt fall away. I rocked my hips forward to meet his mouth.

One savage lick of his miracle tongue and an orgasm tore through me, flooding me with bliss. My guys held me in place, kept me on my feet even though my legs turned to jelly, and my body thrummed, pounding in time with my heart, as I gushed out my bliss into Fen's waiting mouth.

"Yes, gods! Yes!" I gasped.

Grey didn't even stop his soft and sensuous ministrations on the side of my face as he gently removed my torn shirt and bra.

I threw a leg up on Fen's shoulder and Fen lifted the

other, planting his face in my thighs as he dove deep into my folds. His miracle tongue, moving over and within me, induced residual spikes of bliss from my font of pleasure, and that first orgasm didn't recede at all but just kept building.

The three of them moved me carefully to the bed and laid me down with my hips perched on the edge as Fen continued his oral assault on my slit and clit. Ramsey and Grey lay to either side of me, one capturing my lips, while the other delved down to pleasure my breasts.

My hands grasped around frantically until I found their cocks. Grey's was thick, hard, and long. Ramsey had that impossibly thick monstrosity. I stroked them both viciously, wanting them to feel as good as I did.

Grey's devouring mouth held mine in a deep kiss, my body half-lifted to turn to him and Ramsey reached over me to continue fondling my breasts.

"When Fen's done," he whispered in my ear, "do I get to try for twins?"

He had to wait for a response until Gray's hungry lips had been sated and I could turn to him.

"No," I whispered back, teasing my lips across his, but not fully kissing him. "My pussy's off limits to you, you've already filled me up twice, let the others have a chance. But..." I nibbled on his lips. "That means my ass is all yours."

He grinned. "You sure, Silverlocks? With me in your ass you won't be able to stop coming."

"That's the idea," I moaned, pulling his head closer with my hands to deepen our kiss.

And I was so very ready to get started, but there was one last consideration. When I returned to Grey, my voice starting to get hoarse from panting and gasping, I asked him, "We're going to make a mess on your bed. Should we move?"

"Nope, not if you're comfortable. I know a few daemons who could clean it, and if not, I've got a spare in storage."

*Another one?* But I wasn't going to question the odd habits of billionaires.

"Then you really need to get your cock in my pussy," I whispered to him, brushing my lips over his as I spoke. I knew wonderful, patient Fen wouldn't mind being second in line.

We all shifted. Grey lay on the bed, and I straddled him. I took my time teasing his heavy cock around my messy folds before accepting him inside me.

I was so worked up from Fen's miracle tongue that Grey's thick cock slid in easily, and I wiggled my hips, swaying and moving him around inside me as I slowly lowered myself on him.

Then, as I let my weight settle on his hips, feeling him brushing my sacred depths, filling me fully and perfectly, I simply sat there for a long moment, relishing the feel of him inside me.

The way he looked up at me, with such devotion and longing, made me love him all the more. His hands on my hips slid up to my breasts, caressing and pressing with reverence.

He supported me as I leaned down until I was pressed to him and our lips met and mingled in a slow and sensual kiss.

I gasped into his mouth as Ramsey thrust a thick digit into my puckered opening, sending tingling waves of pleasure rolling up my spine. I could simply let my sex aspect get me all worked up and ready for him, but I didn't want to rush this. I wanted him to work for it. And I wanted to feel all of that glorious work myself.

I didn't shift or move on Grey. I simply wanted to feel his full length inside me as we kissed and caressed. He was every bit the attentive lover. His hands brushed lightly to tease, ratcheting up my desire, while Ramsey's fingers swirled and probed and played until I was — hopefully — ready for his uber-XXXL cock.

But when Ramsey did press his massive tip on my opening, it felt impossible. He seemed everywhere around me, leaning over me and Grey, hot against my back. Then, with a single push — which jarred me into Grey, mashing us together — Ramsey opened me fully and slid inside.

I made noises then. Noises I couldn't describe. Very un-lady-like noises. Heavy, guttural, unfathomable noises.

Ramsey chuckled as he once again rose behind me. "Gods, Silverlocks, you really like this, don't you? And I've only got my tip inside you."

His hands clamped to my hips as he moved the head of his massive cock around inside me.

I squirmed and mewled.

*Fuck me!* Only his tip?

He felt like he was filling me completely. But then he pushed in deeper, and I found out what that *truly* felt like.

"Ughhhh, ohhhhhhh, Gods!" I moan-cried as more and more, inch after inch, slowly glided into me.

Finally, after an agonizingly blissful moment, his hips pressed against my cheeks. My breath caught. It was too much. I was too full. And even as I thought that, an orgasm rolled through me, shivering from the top of my head down to my pussy and back up again. I clamped around Grey's cock, moaning and squirming with pleasure.

Gods, Ramsey had been right. With him in my ass, I couldn't stop coming.

I couldn't speak. This was too much sensation, an overload of blissful shudders and contractions and oh! So, I connected with Grey and gasped into his soul: *push me up*.

He shifted me slowly and, between him and Ramsey, they got me to a mostly sitting position.

But every adjustment only made the two cocks inside me press in even more pleasurable ways, which ramped up my orgasmic release. My body shuddered uncontrollably, tears leaked from my eyes and my mouth uttered silent prayers. Ramsey had to hold me to keep me from falling forward, his hands firmly on my tits, as he kissed my neck and shoulders. Then... blessed gods... he began thrusting into my ass.

Grey had a limited range of movement, but still managed to thrust up into me with wet, slapping splashes as I came over and over again.

For the first time, I understood what the guys must feel like with their endless releases. I was trapped at the utmost pinnacle of a perfect orgasm — not a bad place to be trapped at all — as I kept releasing a flood over Grey.

I could barely breathe with the intensity of this pleasure. But then, some tiny voice in the back of my head asked, *wait... if I'm a goddess of sex, shouldn't I be able to experience this glorious, ongoing, perfect pleasure and still remain in control of myself?*

And as if that simple revelation unlocked some next level of my aspect, I returned to myself, still hyper-stimulated but no longer locked in a breathless, wordless haze.

"Fuck yeah," I breathed, finally taking control.

I reached up to take one of Ramsey's hands and slid it down to my clit... because why not! At the same time, I matched his quick thrusts, rocking my hips over him and Grey in undulations which caused both men to gasp.

With a grin, I turned my head to meet Ramsey's lips in a desperate kiss.

"I can't stop coming and I love it," I moaned into his mouth. "Keep it up, big boy."

Grey's hands, planted on my hips, gave him extra leverage as he joined our three-way movement and thrust harder into me. His face was twisted in bliss, even as his eyes kept a lock on me, drinking me in with his void.

Ramsey kissed my neck and shoulders as I looped my hands around behind his head like I had when teasing Grey to get his void to come out. I rocked myself harder on them, feeling every glorious, hard inch of these two powerful men.

One of Grey's hands left my hips to slide up my sweat-slicked body to a breast, clasping as his thrusts grew ragged inside me. His eyes darkened, his void deepening, and his lips opened as he started to shake and lose control.

And gods, it was so fucking sexy to see a man who was always so controlled and calm, driven mad with desire... *for me.*

"I want to feel you come," I gasped to Grey, locking our gazes through two sets of heavily lidded eyes. I could barely hear myself speak over the thundering intensity of my thrashing heart. "Let go. Lose control. Take me!" I begged him.

Except he held onto one last thread of restraint, teasing out this exquisite moment.

Fuck it. If he wouldn't allow himself to fully let go, I'd make him. I surged my sex aspect down into my pussy. My slippery sheath grasped his rigid shaft, then I pushed my aspect past my barriers, into him, filling his cock with sex before adding a touch of fertility for good measure.

"Gods! Ohhh! Yesssss!" Grey cried out, his cock swelling with the hot surge of his release.

It only occurred to me then that I probably hadn't needed to use my fertility aspect as he was already super-potent. But I had to admit, feeling the hot flood of his cum inside of me made me feel that much sexier and more powerful.

And it was a good thing I'd regained my lucidity a moment before, as I was able to use my fertility aspect and ensure everything flowed smoothly. I opened myself to Grey's tidal wave release and urged it deeper within me.

My own, ongoing, orgasmic contractions pushed it along, through and past my womb, to the waiting egg. With my hyper-acuity, I focused all of Grey's sperm on one egg and felt it succumb and breach. I made sure the other egg remained untouched, then withdrew my attentions there to fully enjoy the continued pleasures of my body, and the renewed bliss pulsing through me with Grey's extended — and oh so powerful— release.

"Fuuuuuuck!" Grey drew out the word as his cock pulsed again and again in the throes of his orgasm.

"Yes," I whispered, licking my lips. "Hell yes. You are so fucking incredible!" I slowly lowered myself down over him, until I could whisper in his ear. "You've impregnated me, my potent daemon lord."

He growled another long, "Fuck," and his cock pulsed hard with a renewed wave of bliss.

I gave a breathy laugh, levering myself up onto my arms so I could watch Grey's expression as he came.

My extended, extreme high was ebbing just a little,

and Ramsey, perhaps sensing my need for a break, had stopped his thrusting, simply laying deep within me, throbbing. That was still amazing, but with Grey finally coming down I had a moment to regain myself.

"You guys are too much," I breathed, then closed my eyes and shiver-sighed as Grey's hands came up to casually caress my breasts. "I almost blacked out from too much pleasure."

Ramsey chuckled. "There's more to come."

Oh... I knew. Which made me wonder where Fen had gone. I looked around and saw my glorious blond godling lying on the corner of the bed, smiling at me as he slowly stroked himself.

"You're so fucking gorgeous," he whispered. His aqua-blue gaze held mine. That's what I loved about Fen. Even when I had two other guys inside me that look from him made me feel like we were the only two people in the world.

"You're next," I mouthed to him, and I reached into my love aspect and spoke to him within his soul, privately. *I'm going to make you come so hard you'll fill me up completely and I won't have a choice, I'll have to conceive.*

His long cock twitched and swelled, his eyes going wide, and his hand moved away from his shivering shaft as he breathed through his teeth.

I blew him a kiss with a mischievous grin.

Looking down at Grey as his release finally began to ebb, I connected with his soul. *I want you in my mouth, my love.*

That got his attention, and he nodded and began to move.

"Ramsey, lift me," I commanded and his massive, strong hands reached around me, grabbing my legs and lifting me off Grey. The beautifully tanned man slid out from under us. Ramsey held me in place easily, and I squirmed around Ramsey's huge cock, drawing a low, throaty chuckle.

"Tease," he hissed, his soft, deep voice, and hot breath on my ear and cheek sending thrills through me.

"You love it," I hissed back.

"I do."

Fen knelt before me, taking a moment to kiss me softly, his hands roaming over my sweaty form.

"There aren't words to describe you," he whispered, leaning close, to the opposite side of my face from Ramsey. "Beyond beautiful." He brushed a soft kiss on my cheek. "Lavishly and luxuriously lovely." He nibbled on my earlobe as his whispered words penetrated me. "Sumptuously sublime." The flick of a tongue on my hot neck. "Exquisitely elegant. Delightfully dazzling. Resplendent and ravishing."

I couldn't help but tilt my head as he focused on my neck and ear. I shivered, my eyes filled with loving tears as his words alone almost made me orgasm.

"None of these are enough," he breathed. "You're on another level entirely, my goddess."

Holy. Fucking. Wow!

"Fen," I breathed.

I didn't know what to say and words didn't seem enough for what he'd just given me, so I opened my love aspect.

For a moment, I hesitated, trembling before I connected with him. I'd been terrified of truly loving someone and losing myself in that union, but Fen... Fen was everything I needed and more.

Taking the plunge, I opened my love fully to him, feeling the bright, blasting aura of Fen's adoration for me. That immensity of love brought more tears to my eyes, and I accepted it into me and made sure he could feel my own affection.

Fen gasped and pulled back, eyes wide.

"Ana," he breathed. "Yes! I do!"

*I do?*

Had we just gotten metaphorically married?

*Ah... fuck it, why not.* I laughed lightly. Every girl dreamed of getting married with another guy's huge throbbing cock deep in their ass, right?

I reached out and softly took Fen's face in both hands, bringing his lips to mine in a long, soft and sumptuous, kiss.

"Give me a child, my wonderful wolf," I murmured, and he grinned.

"As you wish, my love."

And I felt it. I felt the fundamental *truth* in those words: *my love.*

He shifted in, adjusting himself to slip his long cock into me, filling me perfectly. Ramsey released me, but I didn't shift much. I was held firm, crushed between these two kneeling men.

A tremor of expectant bliss ran through me, during the moment of stillness before they began to move. When they did — Fen with slow, long thrusts and Ramsey with heavy, slapping lunges — I moaned so unabashedly loud and guttural it made my men chuckle.

"That's my girl. Moan for me," Ramsey said kissing the opposite ear to the one Fen had been kissing a moment ago.

So, I did it again, which was easy, given what I was feeling. These two powerful men possessed me, pressing and fucking with crushing need.

Fen dipped in, kissing and licking my aching breasts, which elicited even more, very un-lady-like moans.

Grey stood on the bed, striding up to my side, gently stroking his cock. He'd just finished a moment ago, but already he was near to fully aroused again.

I reached out and pushed his hand away so I could stroke him. I squeezed his shaft in several slow plunges before bringing him to my lips and licking his tip, tasting our mingled releases.

As I did, I sent a bit of healing and sex into him. His cock leaped to life, instantly full again, growing in my hands. With a smile, I looked into his sable eyes — which were gazing intently down at me — and slowly took him fully into my mouth. His rigid shaft resisted, bending down my throat, but I forced him deeper until my lips were pressed to his base.

Grey let out a shuddering growl as I swallowed several times, contracting my throat around him, squeezing him.

One of his hands came to the back of my head, combing through my hair, not pressing me closer, simply needing to connect with me. The last time I'd had a man this deep in my mouth, I'd discovered my lack of a gag reflex. It seemed my sex aspect had evolved even more since then, as I could now breathe normally around him. And while I kept him there. I sought out with my love aspect as I had with Fen a moment ago.

I felt Grey's carefully guarded emotions, each in its own little box, tucked away and carefully managed... except for his affection for me.

His love blazed forth within him, a warm and heady glow, which filled his soul. Just feeling the full extent of his adoration for me, brought tears to my eyes, and I merged my love with his, hearing his breath catch.

"Yes, Ana!" he gasped softly, "Yes. I do!"

And that was symbolic marriage number two.

Still with another man in my ass.

I pulled slowly off Grey's cock until he was just filling my mouth, then began to suck and play my tongue over his tip while his hand in my hair continued to stroke and caress.

Words weren't needed now. We knew how the other felt.

Fen's pace picked up, hard and constant, his long cock pumping into my permanently pleasured pussy, and

Ramsey's thrusts grew savage. He grunted with each powerful blow and my ass would probably be bruised tomorrow from his constant slams into me, but I could heal that.

This... *this* had been what I'd wanted. What I'd *needed.* All three of my men inside me, devoted and dedicated, focused on me, while also taking what they needed.

*Yeeeeesssss!* My breathy voice echoed into each of their souls and I gave myself over into their hands, trusting them implicitly.

Their pace built in unison, a perfect merging of bodies. Ramsey pounded a solid rhythm of quick short thrusts, timed to match the wild beating of my heart. His strong hands, hard on my hips, kept me in place.

For every two of Ramsey's hard slaps, Fen gave a single lunge, grinding his loins against my clit. That magical tongue of his swirled over my breasts, capturing ragingly hard nipples and squeezing every ounce of exquisite pleasure from them, one, then the other, then back.

Grey had taken control of his thrusts, long, slow plunges of his cock into my throat, and I moved my other hand from his shaft down to cup his sack, feeling its swaying weight. I massaged him as both of his hands fisted in my hair.

And with that culmination of their efforts, my pleasure built to new heights, my need tightening into what threatened to be an earth-shattering orgasm.

I moaned heavily around Grey's cock as a shiver of that orgasm flowed through me, shooting me higher and higher into a divine ecstasy.

Then Ramsey's thrusts became ragged and even more savage. His hot gasps on my neck were rough and uneven. He released a tell-tale chuckle before his torn voice echoed what I'd said earlier.

"Too much!"

But I didn't want him to come yet, so I sent my sex aspect into his cock and held his release.

He gave a long, guttural groan, his entire body twitching against my back.

*Not yet,* I whispered into his soul. But I did want to give him something, so, as I had with the other two, I opened my love to him.

His love was like a wildfire, burning out of control inside him, consuming him and replenishing him in equal measure. In that instant... I knew. I knew that very first time — after our first, powerful sexual encounter — when he'd said the words, "I love you," he'd meant them. I'd broken something open inside of him that he hadn't been ready to admit, but had been raging within him ever since.

*Oh... wow,* I breathed into his soul. Then I shared my love with him, and like a whipping wind, it only blasted his flames hotter and higher.

"I do," he grunt-muttered, then he couldn't stop repeating it. His body shook violently behind me with his held release.

And that made three figurative marriages... this time *with* the guy in my ass.

Except I felt something slightly different with Ramsey. Sex, for him, was the purest and most essential expression of his love, and I was keeping him from fully expressing it by holding his release.

*I'm sorry, Ramsey, just hold on a little longer.* I kissed his soul with the words.

He let out a pained grunt, but inside he whispered, *Yes, mistress.*

Then he stopped thrusting, and held still, his cock quivering, swollen and ready to burst inside me.

I turned my soul-voice to Fen. *It's time, my love. Give me your all. Every last drop.*

I gave his cock the lightest, feathery stroke with my sex aspect. I didn't want to control him, just urge him on. I wanted this to be all him.

His mouth pulled from my chest as he leaned back. His hands lowered, to just above Ramsey's, grasping my waist as his thrusts became savage, pounding into me.

Ramsey grunted in pain, probably feeling every one of Fen's hard thrusts shifting against him inside me and still unable to release.

Fen's head lolled back, and he let out a feral cry as he drove himself into me, slamming hard against my clit, and spiking my bliss to heavenly reaches with each crushing contact.

A hard-gripping, body-shuddering orgasm swept

through me, and my pussy contracted around Fen's cock, milking and needful.

*Now!* I cried out into his soul as my pleasure blasted me into the ether.

Fen drove in, planting himself firmly in my depths as his cock twitched and seemed to super harden, swelling within me as his wolf let out a roar from his lips. Then his heated rush surged into me, pulse after long, hot pulse of torrential flow.

*Yes,* I whispered into Fen's soul, over and over. I kept his wolf at bay, while allowing its feral and savage nature to possess Fen, because wow, that was just too sexy.

I was nearly lost to pleasure but had just enough of a mind to tweak my fertility aspect and ensure everything met and merged within me. A third conception, another child.

Grey cried out as his balls contracted and he pumped his sweet heat into my mouth. He tasted like salty caramel, and I savored his flavor before swallowing every last drop, only to have him fill my mouth again.

And only then did I unleash Ramsey. *Let me have it, big boy,* I screamed into his soul as I released my restraint on him.

Ramsey cried out with a savage grunt as his volcano of a cock erupted with a monumental release. His explosion shook me physically and spiritually. My mind broke and I was torn from my body by the force of a renewed and transcendent orgasm.

Time stopped as I had another out-of-body experience. I saw a static image of the four of us, locked in utmost bliss.

Fen bent back in a feral pose, still somehow gentle, no claws pricking me this time.

Ramsey was all power, body curled around me possessively, eyes wide, mouth gaping.

Grey had his eyes squeezed tight, a tear escaping from his long beautiful lashes.

And I was held in the middle of them, their goddess, their focus, being worshiped... exactly how I wanted to be worshiped.

I wrapped my ethereal self around the scene, spreading a warm embrace over us all. Just like how my guys surrounded me physically, I in turn surrounded them spiritually.

*Thank you,* I breathed into their souls before returning to my body.

The pounding pleasure possessed me again and I let myself go, riding the rapids of this incredible rush as it flowed on and on and on.

I came to myself, laying on top of Fen, who was awkwardly bent back over his legs but didn't seem to care. Ramsey was heavy on my back and Grey had collapsed next to us. We were all still panting hard.

No one spoke. There was nothing to say. We'd expressed everything we'd wanted to.

Slowly, carefully, eventually, we drew apart and Ramsey rose and began drawing a bath in the oversized tub. Sometimes I forgot how thoughtful he could be.

Grey pulled on a robe and left, returning with several couch cushions. Making a few trips, he laid them all out in a large makeshift bed on the floor.

Fen carried me to the massive tub and sat with me as the flow of warm water rose around us. Ramsey had a quick shower and I watched, loving how the water flowed over his huge frame. He was done by the time the tub was full, then he joined us and bathed me with Fen's help. Grey came in and showered, and again I watched the water cascade off his tall, perfect form.

When we were all clean and warm, they carried me back to the new bed and the four of us curled up together. Ramsey behind me, Fen in front but lower, his head just below my breasts, and Grey behind Fen but curled around so we were face to face. Who needed blankets when you were covered in hot men? They teased me with soft kisses as I began to doze, filled with happiness and love and peace: the perfect way to fall asleep.

"ANA? ANAIS?"

I woke, drowsy and so very contented.

Who'd spoken?

It... hadn't been any of my guys. They were all still asleep, close around me. And... the voice had been feminine.

"Ana?" Harmonia asked as she peeked around the

door to Grey's room. She was simultaneously trying to get my attention while not looking at us.

"Harmonia? What time is it?"

She blinked as if that were a silly question. "Ah... I don't know, three or four? I need to speak to you... now. And not in here."

I gave a soft laugh and rose, carefully extricating myself from my amazing lovers. I found a robe and slipped it on before joining Harmonia in the hall and she led me back to the main living area.

"What is it?" I asked.

She seemed distracted and agitated, looking around quickly, making sure we were alone.

"Ana," she whispered. "I know who your mother is."

Don't miss the next book in the series!

**Claiming Demons**

The Secret Gods Keep: Book Three

***My name is Ana Baker... and I'm a goddess?***

I still don't believe it, but everyone keeps telling me it's true.

And putting a name to all my strange powers still hasn't helped me figure out who I am.

But, when my best friend discovers who my birth mother is, I start to hope I can begin to understand myself a bit better.

Not that I'm complaining, I have three sexy daemon princes who are madly in love with me. Grey, a pillar of order and sanity in my otherwise chaotic life. Ramsey, a sexy beast of a man who'll always protect me. And Fen, my sweet-talking confidante with a miracle tongue. And what's great is that they've finally started to get along!

But when a conclave of the gods draws all new celestials to town, things get complicated once again. Grey's sister, Erini, is out for my blood, Fen's father Loki is up to his old mischief, and Ramsey's cousin Horus wants to claim me as his bride.

Luckily, I'm a goddess and I can take care of myself... probably...

## OTHER BOOKS BY TESSA COLE

### NEPHILIM'S DESTINY

*Destined Shadows, prequel story*

*Destined Darkness, book 1*

*Destined Blood, book 2*

*Destined Fire, book 3*

*Destined Storm, book 4*

*Destined Radiance, book 5*

### ANGEL'S FATE

*Fated Bonds, book 1*

*Fated Winter, book 2*

*Fated Fear, book 3*

*Fated Despair, book 4*

*Fated Resolve, book 5*

*Fated Heart, book 6*

### ENSNARED BY THE PACK

*Wolf Deceived, book 1*

*Wolf Denied, book 2*

*Wolf Desired, book 3*

*Wolf Distressed, book 4*

*Wolf Decided, book 5*

*Wolf Devoted, book 6*

**THE GRECIAN GODDESS TRILOGY**

**Co-written with Clara Wils**

*Kiss of the Goddess, book 1*

*Power of the Goddess, book 2*

*Bonds of the Goddess, book 3*

**THE SECRETS GODS KEEP**

**Co-written with Clara Wils**

*Craving Demons, book 1*

*Chaos Demons, book 2*

*Claiming Demons, book 3*

## OTHER BOOKS BY CLARA WILS

**THE GRECIAN GODDESS TRILOGY**

**Co-written with Clara Wils**

*Kiss of the Goddess, book 1*

*Power of the Goddess, book 2*

*Bonds of the Goddess, book 3*

**THE MISTS OF ELISTA TRILOGY**

*Bonds and Blood, book 1*

*Shape and Shadows, book 2*

*Form and Fury, book 3*

**SISTER SPIRITS**

*Double Discover, book 1*

*Double Danger, book 2*

*Double Disaster, book 3*

*Double Doom, book 4*

*Double Destiny, book 5*

**THE SECRETS GODS KEEP**

**Co-written with Clara Wils**

*Craving Demons, book 1*

*Chaos Demons, book 2*

*Claiming Demons, book 3*

www.ingramcontent.com/pod-product-compliance
Lightning Source LLC
LaVergne TN
LVHW091038080826
845145LV00002B/536

*9781990587313*